BATTLING TROY

Devil's Knights Series
Book 4

Winter Travers

Amanda,

Enjoy Troy & Marley!

1

Table of Contents

Dedication

For my Mom and Dad.
The two greatest people I will ever know.
Thank you for loving and supporting me.

Acknowledgements

So many things changed while writing this book. Thank you to everyone who stood by me. Your unwavering support amazes me every day.

Wood, Carter, Mom, Dad, Jenny, Andy, Adam, Jamie, my amazing nieces and nephews, Lizette (Awesome PA), Karla, Chelsie, Brandi, and everyone else I know I'm missing, THANK YOU!

BATTLING TROY

Chapter 1

Marley

This was ridiculous. I was the victim of the most disorganized kidnapping ever. Not only had a mesh sack been thrown over my head, (Hello! It was mesh, idiots!) But my hands had been tied together with neon pink shoelaces.

"How the hell do those Knights get all the hot puntas?" the one with a red hat on asked.

"Not a fucking clue, hombre. All I know is I plan on having a taste of this punta before we get rid of her." The one with a buzz cut said, as he licked his lips and puckered his lips at me.

Ew. I shivered in disgust and focused on how to get the hell out of here. I had gathered from what they had been saying that they thought I was Cyn. These morons had apparently never seen Cyn because Cyn and I were complete opposites. You would have to be blind to confuse us. Or an Assassin apparently.

"I'm sure Big A will want the first crack at her," Red Hat said.

OK, time to think. I didn't want anyone getting first 'crack' at me. "Um, hi," I said, getting their attention.

"Look, the punta muñequita speaks," Buzzcut sneered.

"Um, I gather that you two think I'm Cyn," I stated, getting straight to the point. "But I'm not."

They both threw their heads back, laughing. "You *are* Cyn."

Oy. These guys were idiots. "No, I'm actually not. I have no connection to the Knights." I was not about to tell them I was Gravel's daughter. They might let me go if they thought I had nothing to do with the Knights.

"Then what were you doing leaving the clubhouse? Are you one of their puntas?" Red Hat said, his eyes traveling up and down my body.

Ugh. Double ew. "I was just there for the party. I only met Rigid for a minute. He's not going to care what happens to me."

"We don't believe you, punta. You will say anything for us to let you go," Buzzcut said, advancing on me.

"I send you on a simple task of grabbing Cyn and instead you come back with some random punta?"

I look over my shoulder and see a short, Hispanic man enter the room, glaring at Buzz cut and red hat. I turned my gaze back to the two idiots and smirked at them. Ha!

"We did what you asked, jefe," Red Hat said, taking his hat off and held it to his chest.

"I asked you to grab some random Punta?"

"Well, no. You asked for us to grab Rigid's mujer. We saw her talking to him earlier in the night and figured she had to be Cyn," Buzzcut explained, trying to dig himself out of the hole he was in.

"God help me," Shorty said, as he walked over to me and crouched down. "You're not Cyn, are you?" he asked me.

"Nope," I said, popping the p. "I was trying to tell tweedle dee and tweedle dumb here that, but they didn't believe me."

He shook his head and stood up, turning his back to me. "Untie her and drop her off somewhere. She isn't going to be any help to us."

"We can't just let her go!" Red hat yelled.

"She's seen our faces, boss," Buzzcut chimed in.

"I don't care. I'm not going to hurt some niña because you fucking idiots grabbed the wrong girl. Do it now," he ordered, turning around and walked out of the room.

"Ala chingada," Red Hat said, walking over to me and started untying my arms.

"You know who Cyn is?" Buzz cut asked me, getting in my face.

"No. That was my first time at the clubhouse. Now let me go. I can't help you, asshole."

"You sure are a punta. I ought to teach you a lesson." He spit at me.

"Knock it off, Jose, and help me get her back in the van."

"Oh, I'll knock something off," Buzzcut said, standing up and sneering down at me.

He reared back, winding up his fist. The last thing I remembered was his fist connecting with my face and thinking that was going to leave a mark.

--*-*-*-*-*-*-*-*-*-*-*-*

15

Chapter 2

TROY

"If we don't find her, I'm stringing you up by your balls and leaving you for dead," Gravel threatened for the tenth time as he threw his leg over his bike and took off in a cloud of dust.

I took my hat off and ran my fingers through my hair. Big A from the Assassins had just called and told King that they were dropping Marley off somewhere. He didn't tell King where, because Big A was under the impression that Marley was nobody to the Knights.

King had let him believe that she was just some club pussy they had accidently kidnapped. As soon as everyone had heard that they were turning Marley loose, they had all taken off looking for her.

"You riding with me?" Meg asked, walking out of the clubhouse.

"King is actually letting you go look for Marley?" I asked, surprised.

"Phff. I do what I want," Meg said, swinging her door open.

"I find that hard to believe," I said, opening the passenger door and sliding in next to her.

"OK, OK I begged and pleaded and promised him you would go with me," she confessed, backing out of her parking spot. She shifted into drive, and we rocketed out of the parking lot.

"Do you even know where we are going?" I asked, as I reached over my shoulder and grabbed the seat belt.

"Around."

"Around? Really? Do you think we are just going to stumble upon her?" I asked, snapping the buckle in place.

"I have a couple of ideas, but my main plan is to drive around and look in places where it would be good to dump a body."

"Dump a body? Really, Meg? I think it's safe to say that Marley is fine. We just need an idea where they are dropping her off."

"That's what I meant, dropping her off," she replied, whipping around a back alley and rolled her window down.

"Do you think you could drive without giving me whiplash?" I asked, rubbing my neck.

"Toughen up cupcake," Meg said, careening out of the alley and back on the street.

I looked up and down every alley and driveway we passed but didn't see anything.

"Did you actually sleep with Marley last night?"

"Uh, well, we really didn't do a lot of sleeping," I smirked.

"You're such a pig." Meg rolled her eyes.

"Hey, you asked."

"So, do you like her?" She asked, looking over at me.

Do I like Marley? That was an understatement. On top of her being drop dead gorgeous, she had one hell of a wicked sense of humor. It was hard to find a girl who had the same laid-back personality as I had and also is funny. The few hours I had spent with Marley had been fantastic.

"She's a cool chick," I replied, not wanting to give too much away. I knew how Meg was. She and I had been friends for years, and I knew how she worked. She was pumping me for information right now, and I knew she was plotting in her head.

"Really, just a cool chick?"

"Yup," I shook my head and continued staring out the window, hoping to see something that would distract Meg from her interrogation.

"So do you plan on seeing her again?"

"Guess that all depends on if we find her or not."

"We will. I'm going to head to the gas station and fill up. King drove my truck and didn't fill it up," Meg griped, whipping a shitty and heading back the way we came.

"Was that Gravel that just drove by?" I asked, watching a motorcycle whiz by us.

Meg glanced in her side mirror and smiled at me. "You mean your future father-in-law?" She laughed.

"You're such a bitch sometimes, you know that?"

"I know. You tell me, at least, two times a day at work," she smirked, turning into the gas station and pulling up to a pump.

"I'll pump if you just want to swipe your card," I said, opening my door.

"Hell yeah. You know I hate pumping gas," she said, getting out and walked over to the pump. She swiped her card and headed into the gas station. I could only imagine what she was buying.

I started pumping the gas and leaned against the truck, watching the numbers go up. The numbers whizzed by as I thought about Marley and what the hell was going to happen once we found her.

I had initially thought of calling her, but after I found out she was Gravel's daughter, that kind of stopped me in my tracks. I know Meg was fully immersed in the MC world, but I don't know if that is something I want. I had helped out when the whole thing with asshat and Cyn had gone down, but I only did it because of Cyn.

Last night with Marley had definitely been awesome, but was it better to be left as a one-night thing now that I knew more about her? Gravel was convinced I was trying to get with Meg. I absolutely, under no doubt, did not like Meg more than friends. She was like a freaking sister to me. I treated her like one of the guys. Half the fucking time I forgot she even was a chick.

"Dude, you are not going to believe what I just bought. They had deep fried cheese that is covered in crushed-up nacho cheese Doritos. I fucking *love* Wisconsin," Meg said, handing me a small cardboard box. I peeked through the window on top and saw four neon orange triangles.

"Are you sure these are edible?" I asked, opening the box and sniffing them.

"Dude, it's cheese. Of course, it's edible," Meg said, reaching in and grabbing one.

The gas pump clicked off, and I handed the box back to Meg. "We need to get back on the road looking for Marley," I said, hanging the nozzle back up.

"I know, I just needed to get something to eat. I was starving," Meg said, cramming another mutant nacho cheese thing in her mouth.

"I'll drive." I grabbed the keys that were dangling from her fingertips and walked around the truck to the driver's side.

"You better be thankful I have my hands full right now. Otherwise, I'd punch you in the junk, ass," Meg said, sliding in on the other side and setting her bounty of snacks from the store in between us.

"So thankful. I don't want to end up like Hunter," I smirked, starting the truck and heading out of the parking lot.

"Ugh, please don't mention Hunter, you'll ruin my appetite."

"Have you seen him since you punched him?" I asked, laughing. I still love when Meg tells the story of how she punched Hunter in the junk when he hit on her. I only wish I could have been there to see it. I had actually been friends with Hunter first and met Meg through him. Meg and I had started working together and then I had begun to see how Hunter really was. He always told his friends that Meg was the issue and was anti-social, but after working with her for a couple months, I started to see the real Hunter.

"No, thankfully I have not seen the douche king. Remy said he was limping for a couple of hours after it, but that's all I heard," Meg said as she grabbed her huge ass drink off the floor that she had wedged between her feet.

"Give me one," I said, seeing there were only two mutant orange triangles left. Half the time I had to fight Meg to get food. Another reason I never thought of her as a girl, she was a fucking bottomless pit. She handed me one and shoved the other one in her mouth.

"Go to her house, maybe they dropped her off there," Meg said around a mouthful.

I crammed the mutant orange triangle into my mouth and instantly moaned. Son of a bitch that was some good cheese.

"Good, right?" Meg asked, a huge smile on her face.

"Yeah, yeah, you were right again. You can't go wrong when it comes to cheese," I mumbled.

"Turn down Allan and then Chester and Marley is the third house on the left."

"What the hell else did you buy?" I asked as I watched Meg rummage through the plastic bag.

"Licorice, three candy bars, and a bag of shrimp."

"Fucking shrimp?!"

"Yeah, I thought I could make Lo some shrimp stir fry tonight," she said as she put the bag on the floor by her feet.

Meg just bought fucking shrimp from a gas station. A. Fucking. Gas. Station.

"Are you trying to poison King?" I asked, turning down Chester.

"You're a jackass," Meg pouted. She crossed her arms over her chest and kicked the bag on the floor.

"Yeah, and you're a fucking loon half the time."

"Now I have to think of something else to make for dinner."

"You can make him shrimp stir-fry, I just wouldn't use shrimp from a fucking gas station."

Meg huffed and turned to look out the side window. "Slow down, her house is on the left." I slowed down and pulled over to the curb in front of her house just as Meg's cell phone started ringing.

I glanced at Marley's house, seeing that she lived only a little bit away from Ethel. I don't know if I would want to live that close to the woman who was banging my dad.

"Wait!" Meg said, grabbing my arm as I reached for the door handle. "Head back to downtown," Meg said to me, the phone still held to her ear.

"Why? Do we know where she is?" I asked, staring at Meg.

"Just drive. You are not going to believe this shit," Meg said, ending her phone call and shoving her phone into her pocket.

"Tell me where the fuck we are going," I demanded as I cranked up the truck and made a u-turn to head back the way we had just come.

"They know where Marley is."

"And?"

"Head to Curl Up and Dye."

"What the fuck?"

"Marley broke a nail, and she headed there to get it fixed," Meg said, a grin spreading across her lips.

"That was her first thought after being released from kidnappers? The fucking nail salon?" I ask, outraged. That was fucking insane.

"Looks like you have your own loon to deal with now," Meg laughed.

I shot Meg an eat shit look but didn't say anything. I wouldn't say Marley was a loon, but she sure had her priorities off I don't know what she was thinking, but I sure as hell knew what I was thinking.

As soon as I got her alone, I was going to tell her exactly what I thought about going to a fucking salon instead of back to the clubhouse. Then her soft firm ass was going to find out what the palm of my hand felt like.

--*-*-*-*-*-*-*-*-*-*-*

Chapter 3

Marley

"I really think you should get that looked at, hun. I don't think you should have that large of a lump on the side of your head. It's bulging," Gwen said as she set the bottle of clear coat nail polish down and gazed worriedly at my head.

"I'll be okay. I'm just waiting for those Tylenol you gave me to kick in." I reached up and gently rubbed the side of my head with the palm of my hand, careful not to smudge the touch-up Gwen had just done.

Big A's dumb as rocks henchmen had thankfully dropped me only two blocks away from the salon. The only smart thing to do was to walk to Curl Up and Dye to call Gravel and then have Gwen fix my manicure while I waited.

I had never been kidnapped before, so I'm not sure what the protocol is, but I'm pretty sure the Assassins missed the mark, big time. I was terrified when tweedle dee and tweedle dumb grabbed me, but as soon as they had opened their mouths in the van, I knew I was the victim of a second rate kidnapping.

I still had no idea how the hell they had thought that I was Cyn. Cyn was all sweet and sexy siren, while, although I hate to admit, I tend to lean more towards Barbie. We were on completely opposite ends of the spectrum.

Thank God King had called when he did, because even though I wasn't afraid of dumb and dumber, Big A scared the shit out of me. He may not look like much of a man, but I could tell there was a coldness behind his eyes that I didn't want to see personally.

"Hell of a thing to happen to you on your day off. There go your plans for finishing unpacking all of those boxes you have in the spare bedroom," Gwen said, putting away everything on her station.

I had come to find out that in the time I had worked at the salon that Gwen was a bit of a neat freak, which really surprised the hell out of me. Gwen was pure rockabilly to the core. A definite throwback to the 1950's. She always wore amazing dresses and the most killer shoes I had ever seen.

Today she had on a black swing dress with tiny red polka dots all over it, and her breasts were barely contained. I had been taken back by her, shall we say, 'breast independence,' when I had first met her. Now I'm pretty sure if I saw her in a turtleneck, I would be shocked.

"So what were you doing last night that got you kidnapped?"

"I was leaving the clubhouse early this morning with fond memories of sleeping in my own bed when dumb and dumber had grabbed me." I held my hand up in front of me and blew on my nails, helping them dry faster.

"You told me that, I meant what, or should I say who, kept you at the clubhouse so late?"

The most amazing guy I had ever met? A guy I wish I would have just stayed in bed with? Mr. Right? Ugh. I seriously didn't know who the fabulous man I spent the night with was, and I doubted I would ever find out. "Just a guy," I said vaguely.

"Well, was this guy worth getting kidnapped over?"

So worth it. Three orgasms worth. "I guess."

"You guess?" Gwen said, resting her hands on her hips. 'I bet-," Gwen started but was cut off by the truck that screeched to halt in front of the salon. I saw Meg hop out of the passenger side and breathed a sigh of relief that it was her that has come to get me and not Gravel. I wasn't up for our strained and awkward relationship.

"Holy hell, who is that tall drink of water?" Gwen asked from behind me.

I shifted my eyes to the driver side, expecting to see King following Meg into the salon, but my jaw dropped when I saw it was Mr. Right from last night. What the hell was he doing with Meg? I had asked him last night if he was part of the club and he had said he wasn't. What a fucking liar. I had seen my own father choose the club over me countless times, and I knew that I did not want to be with a man who had anything to do with the Devil's Knights. Mr. Right had just turned into Mr. Hell No.

"He's all yours," I said, turning away from the front window. As I was standing up, I heard the roar of motorcycles coming down the street, and I knew I wasn't as lucky as I thought I was. Now I had my father here and also the guy I had slept with last night. This might get interesting.

"I'm going to go grab some popcorn and watch the biker show," Gwen said, ducking behind the front reception desk as the front door swung open. Meg and Mr. Hell No walked in and looked around.

I kept my gaze on Mr. Hell No, waiting to see his reaction. It was worth the wait.

His gaze traveled up my body, caressing every inch of me. I fidgeted under his gaze and rubbed my hands on my jeans.

"Holy shit! What happened to your head?" Meg shouted as she walked towards me.

I ripped me gaze off of him and focused on Meg. "It's nothing."

"That sure doesn't look like nothing. It looks like they took a baseball bat to your head. Maybe you should sit down," Meg said, pulling one of the chairs that were pulled up to the manicure station and pushed it towards me.

"I'm fine, promise. I took some Tylenol and just need to rest once I get home."

"The only place you are going is the hospital," Mr. Hell No growled at me.

My eyes opened wide, shocked at his words. Who the hell was he to tell me what I was going to do? He was just a one night stand that I had no plans of revisiting, no matter how tempting he looked right now.

"I told her she should have gone to the hospital instead of here, but she didn't listen," Gwen replied, popping up from behind the reception desk.

"Holy shit," Meg said, jumping back from Gwen. "Where the hell did you come from?"

"I needed snacks," Gwen said, holding up a bag of popcorn she always had stashed and shoved a handful into her mouth.

"Sweet," Meg said, holding her hand out for some. I watched as Meg and Gwen eyed each other up, deciding if the other was alright. From what I knew of Meg, she and Gwen were going to be two peas in a pod. Neither one thought before they spoke and were the life of the party.

"Seriously, you get kidnapped and then they let you go, and this is the first place you go, a fucking salon?" Mr. Hell No thundered at me.

"Hey, look-" I started, but Meg interrupted me.

"Troy, lay off. She's OK," Meg said around a mouthful of popcorn.

Troy? Holy hell, this was Troy? The guy who last night's party was for and the guy I had slept with. Shit. I had to sit down. My head was swimming with the fact Mr. Right had turned into Mr. Hell No and now turned into Troy. Plus, my head really wasn't feeling the greatest. The pills Gwen had given me had barely touched the freight train running through my head.

I pulled the chair to me Meg had offered before and plopped my ass in it. I leaned forward, resting my head on my hands, careful to not hit the huge bump on the side.

"Where the hell is she?" Gravel boomed as he walked through the front door. Oh great, just what I needed, my father added to the shit storm rolling through my head.

"Over here," I mumbled, waving my hand in the air.

"Jesus Christ, Troy. What the hell did you do to her?" Gravel said as he walked over and kneeled down in front of me.

"You're fucking kidding me, right?" Troy said, crossing his arms over his chest.

"He didn't do anything, Gravel. You know that " I said, raising my head to look him in the eye.

"I see my girl hurt, I blame the first guy I see."

"Well, you were fucking wrong with that assumption," Troy shot back.

"You want to know what fucking assumption I'm going to make, smart ass?" Gravel roared, raising up from the floor and getting in Troy's face.

"Oh, this is getting good," Gwen mumbled around a mouth of popcorn. "So who is Troy in all of this?" She asked Meg.

"Troy is who Marley slept with last night and the last person to see her before she got kidnapped this morning. Gravel blames Troy for Marley getting kidnapped," Gwen bugged her eyes out at Meg in disbelief. "Crazy, I know," Meg said.

"That is my daughter, you little cocksucker. I don't even know what the hell you are doing here. You think just because you got your dick wet that you belong somewhere in all of this? Well, you better think twice about that. Marley knows better than to get tangled up with the likes of you," Gravel ranted, his finger pointed in Troy's face.

I closed my eyes, feeling a wave of nausea hit me. Between the shit getting knocked out of me and these two idiots going at, I was about to pass out.

"Um, guys…" Meg trailed off.

"Not now!" Gravel and Troy bellowed at the same time.

I felt my body begin to sway and the floor looking like a good place to lay down.

"Troy!" Meg yelled. I opened my eyes to see Meg pointing at me and both guys turning to look at me. I felt another wave of nausea roll through me and closed my eyes again, willing the rolling of my stomach to stop.

"Holy shit," I heard Troy mumble as I leaned to left, I was fine five minutes ago, and I didn't know what the hell was wrong with me. I felt two strong hands grab onto my shoulders and hold me upright.

"We need to get her to the hospital."

"We can take my truck. I'll drive." I heard Meg say as I heard the jingling of keys.

"Get the door," Troy barked as he slipped his arm under my legs and the other braced my back. He lifted me off the chair and held me to his chest. I wanted to fight him and tell him to put me down, but my head was pounding so furiously now, all I wanted was to fall asleep or pass out.

"I'll call Ethel and have her meet us there," I heard Gravel say as we walked out the front door. I kept my eyes shut, afraid if I opened them, I would lose my stomach all over the sidewalk.

I rested my head against Troy's shoulder and felt him turn to the side and slide into Meg's truck. Someone must have slammed the door shut behind us and then I felt Meg climb in on the driver's side.

"I'll be there in ten minutes," Meg said as I felt her shift the truck into drive and take off.

I groaned as she turned the corner, feeling my stomach starting to revolt.

"Shh, it's OK," Troy mumbled as he brushed my hair out of my face. I nestled my face even more into the crook of his neck and breathed in his scent.

"You think she's going to be OK?" I heard Meg ask.

"Yeah, I think she's just got a bad concussion."

"I just want to sleep," I mumbled.

"No sleeping yet, honey. We need to get to the doctor and have him check you over."

"Hmm, just a little nap. You don't have to tell anyone." I burrowed further into him, trying to crawl into his skin and surround myself with his scent. Man, he smelt good.

Troy mumbled above me, but I couldn't make out what he was saying. My head was swimming, and all I wanted to do was close my eyes. I peeked out of my cocoon to see if Troy was looking at me, and he wasn't. I turned my head back into his neck and breathed a sigh. I shut my eyes, telling myself I wasn't going to fall asleep. I was just going to rest my eyes.

At least, that's what I told myself. I was out in ten seconds.

--*-*-*-*-*-*-*-*-*-*-*

Chapter 4

TROY

"She's got a mild concussion. The Doc doesn't think he needs to hold her overnight. She also has a couple of bruised ribs, but nothing severe." I heard Gravel rumble as I stood behind Meg, Cyn, King, and Rigid.

The second Gravel had walked through the swinging doors of the emergency room, his eyes had zoomed in on me, cutting through me like I was nothing. I had no idea what I had done to him, other than sleep with his daughter. Marley was way past the legal age to have sex, the old man needed to get the stick out of his ass and lay off me.

"Is she going home, or to your house?" Meg asked Gravel.

"Ethel and I think she should stay with us a couple of days. Marley is fighting me tooth and nail about it, but I'm not taking no for an answer."

"All right, can we see her?" Meg asked.

"Yeah, two at a time. Although he might have her released by the time you all make it back there. I heard there was a bus accident on the highway with a lot of injuries, and this is the closest hospital. They are trying to clear out beds to make room."

"I'm going first," Meg said, raising her hand.

"Me too," Cyn said right after Meg.

Meg grabbed Cyn's hand, and they headed down the hall to Marley's room, leaving me with King, Rigid, and Gravel, who was still shooting daggers at me.

"What the fuck are you doing here?"

Oh fuck, here we go. "I came to make sure Marley was OK."

"She's fine, now fucking leave," Gravel said, pointing his hand at the exit behind me.

"I think I'll stay and find out for myself." I crossed my arms over my chest and widened my stance. I wasn't about to let Gravel think that he could scare me away.

"I don't see a fucking point in you being here. Marley has all the family she needs here. She doesn't need a fucking one night stand coming in and checking on her." Gravel took two steps towards me, trying to intimidate me.

I wasn't having any of it. "Why don't we let Marley be the judge of that?"

"Why don't you let my fucking fist be the judge, you fucking prick," Gravel growled, reaching back, winding his arm up.

"Knock it off!" King bellowed, halting Gravel and me.

"I want him out of here," Gravel said, pointing his finger into my chest.

"Touch me again and see what happens." I knocked his hand away and stared him down.

"Knock it off, Lincoln."

Gravel whirled around, and I stepped to the side to see Marley walking down the hall with Meg and Cyn on the sides.

"What are you doing out here?" Gravel and I asked at the same time.

"I'm released. Take me home so I can take a bath and pass out."

"The nurse said you need someone waking you up every couple of hours," Meg said.

"She's coming home with me. Ethel and I can take turns waking her up in the middle of the night."

"Gravel, I really just want to go home and sleep in my own bed. I'll set an alarm for every couple of hours, and I'll be okay. It said it was just a mild concussion."

"Fine, you want your own bed, Ethel and I will come and stay at your house for the night."

"No. I'm not some needy child that needs her father. I've been fine on my own since we moved to California, I don't need you now." Marley hitched her purse up higher on her shoulder and stared her father down.

"I'm not letting you go home alone. Someone needs to stay with you."

"No."

"Yes. That's final."

Marley shifted her eyes over to me, and a smile spread across her lips. Oh fuck, I knew exactly what was coming next.

"You want someone to stay with me, Gravel?"

"Now she finally gets it." Gravel threw his hands up in the air, thinking that he had finally gotten through to Marley.

Her grin grew even wider, and I knew she was about to land the winning punch that was going to blow the wind out of Gravel's sails. "I choose Troy to stay with me then."

Oh shit.

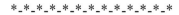

Marley

I watched Gravel's face turn bright red and his fists clenched at his sides. "No."

"It's Troy or nothing," I said, propping my hands on my hips.

"Just come stay at Ethel's house for one god damn night. It's not going to kill you."

"No. I'm going home, and Troy is coming with me, no one else." I stared him in the eye, letting him know I wasn't going to budge on my decision.

I waited for him to say anything else, but he kept quiet, although I could see the veins in his forehead popping out. I didn't want anyone to come home with me, but if I had to choose, I see Troy as my best choice.

"Here, take my truck. I'll ride home with Lo. You can bring back my truck tomorrow." Meg tossed her keys to Troy and smiled.

Troy snatched them out of the air and looked at me. His eyes burned into me, as we both remembered last night. Here I was, standing in a hospital with a mild concussion and all I could think about was the man standing in front of me.

"I already called in for the night off of work, so I'm okay with watching you tonight."

"See, it all works out, Gravel. I'll see you tomorrow." I breezed past Gravel the best I could considering my head was still throbbing and grabbed Troy's hand.

"Don't think I'm OK with this," Gravel yelled at our retreating backs. I gripped Troy's hand tighter as we reached the doors and I got dizzy when we pushed through the doors. I stumbled over the door frame, and Troy wrapped his arm around my waist.

"I'm all for you making your dramatic exit after telling your dad the way things are going to be, but let's not pass out from it."

I looked up into Troy's face, seeing his gray eyes smiling down at me and a smirk playing on his lips. "Don't call him my dad, he's Gravel."

"OK. I must have misunderstood, I thought he was your dad."

"He is in the technical sense." Troy looked at me, questioning what the hell I was talking about. "I'll explain later. Right now, all I want to do is slip into the tub and then pass out in my own bed."

"How about-." Troy started saying but was cut off by the loud grumbling of my stomach. "We'll stop, get something to eat and then work on your bath and passing out." Troy led me to the truck and opened the door.

"How about we stop and get food and then you can just drop me off at my house. I'm going to be fine, I don't need a babysitter." I rested my hand on the door, not getting in until Troy agreed to just drop me off at home.

"No can do. I know for a fact your father and half the club will be driving past your house at some point tonight, checking up on us. I don't want to get my ass kicked for something that I said I would be doing, but I'm not. I said I'll be at your house, so that's where I'm going to be."

"Gah, I totally should have picked Gambler to stay with me," I mumbled as I climbed into the truck and Troy shut the door behind me.

I reached behind me, grabbing the seat belt and groaned as my bruised ribs protested.

"Stop, I got it." Troy reached over, grabbing the seat belt out of my hand and pulled it around me and snapped it into place.

His face was right in front me when he looked up, and our eyes looked at one another. "I could have gotten it."

"I know. I just didn't want you to hurt yourself," he whispered, his lips inches away from me.

"Thanks," I whispered, not knowing what else to say.

Troy pulled away, breaking the trance I was in and started up the truck and pulled out of the parking lot.

"Do you know where I live?"

"Yeah. Meg showed me where when we were looking for you. You're only a couple of houses down from Ethel," Troy said as he maneuvered down the town side streets. I really had no idea where we were going, but I assumed it was to some fast food restaurant. Rockton was a much smaller town than I had ever lived in before, but it was still taking me some time to get used to where everything was.

"You good with Chinese?"

"Sure. Can we just get it to go?"

"Yeah, I'll call in our order." Troy grabbed his phone, swiping to unlock the screen. "Is there anything special you want?"

"Sesame chicken and steamed dumplings." My usual order.

While Troy called for the food, I glanced around, trying to remember the way we were going for future reference. If it wasn't work, the clubhouse, or the grocery store, I had no idea how to get to it.

"It'll be ready in ten minutes." Troy slid his phone into his pocket and turned down another side street. I was completely lost.

"I've never been this way before," I said, looking out the window.

"We're headed over to my house quick. I need to pick up some clothes."

"How long have you lived in Rockton?"

"All my life."

"Wow. I can't imagine living in the same place forever. After my mom and I had left Illinois, we lived in about four different towns before we settled down in Forrest View."

"There's no reason for me to leave Rockton. All my friends and family are here, what else could I need?" Troy asked, glancing over at me. I wish that I had what he had. Leaving my mom and California had been an easy decision, there was nothing there holding me down.

"I didn't really have much of a choice when we moved. Mom and my aunt decided it would be best to get away from everything and start over new."

"Is that why you came back, you missed your dad?"

Ha! Boy was Troy waaay off track. "Hardly. I came back because things in California weren't working out for me."

"You want to wait here, or come inside?" Troy asked as we pulled up in front of a two-story house with an enormous wrap-around porch.

"This is where you live?" I gazed out the windshield, amazed at the vastness and all around awesomeness of

Troy's house. It was the kind of house I always imagined living in.

"For the past seven years."

"You live here all alone?" His house had to have had at least three bedrooms and two bathrooms.

"Yeah. When I first moved in, I rented out the basement to a buddy, but when he got married and moved out, I never looked for another tenant. I like having the whole house to myself now."

"Makes sense."

"You coming in or not?" His hand was on the door handle, waiting for my answer.

"Not. I'll just wait here."

"Suit yourself. I'll be back out in five minutes. I just need to let Bandit out and grab a change of clothes."

"Bandit?" I asked as he opened the door and jumped down from the truck.

"Dog." Troy slammed the door shut and made his way to the front door.

Not only did he have the house of my dreams, but he also had a dog. I had wanted a dog ever since I was eight years old. I had begged and begged my mom that whole year for a dog, but I never got one. She told me we weren't dog people.

I watched as Troy unlocked his front door, pushing it open and was bombarded by an enormous silver lab who was jumping all over Troy begging for attention.

Troy held his hand out, and Bandit instantly stopped jumping around and sat down. I sat forward, intently watching Troy and Bandit.

"Go." Troy pointed to the grass. Bandit got up and moseyed to the lawn and started sniffing around. Troy disappeared into the house and left the door open a crack.

I kept my eyes trained on Bandit, wondering if I could get out quick, pet him, and be back in the truck by the time Troy came back out.

Bandit finished up his business, and I figured it was now or never if I wanted to pet him. I slid out of the truck and slowly made my way over to Bandit.

He was sniffing the trunk of a tree when he heard me behind him. He quick whipped around and started barking. Shit, there went my idea of quick petting him.

"Shh, it's OK, handsome. I just want to pet you," I cooed, holding my hand out for him to sniff.

He stretched out, his paws not moving, but his neck was stretched out trying to smell me. I moved two steps closer and crouched down closer to him, waiting to see if I would pass the sniff test.

His tongue snaked out and licked my hand. He nudged it with his nose, and I took that as my permission to pet him. My fingertips grazed his soft ears, and I knew I had a big loopy smile on my face. I freaking loved dogs.

I plopped down on my knees and started scratching Bandit behind his ears.

"I guess he's not much of a guard dog."

I whipped my head around and saw Troy coming out of the house with a duffle bag tossed over his shoulder.

"He's sweet."

"Huh, he's something alright."

Bandit had sat down and was leaning his head on my hand, begging for more petting.

"OK. That's enough, Bandit. Back in the house." Troy whistled, and Bandit stood up, his tail wagging a mile a minute.

"You're just going to leave him here tonight?"

"I'll have the neighbor come and check on him before bed this evening. He should be fine."

"You can bring him to my house if you want. He's sweet," I said once again.

"You won't want that. Bandit is shameless when it comes to attention and petting. He won't leave you alone the whole night, and you really need to sleep," Troy said, walking to the front door and patted his leg, calling Bandit to go in the house.

"I really want him to come. Please," I begged, shuffling forward on my knees closer to Bandit. I cradled his gorgeous gray head in my hands and placed a kiss on his face.

"Unbelievable."

"What's unbelievable?" I asked as I buried my face in his neck and rubbed his back. Bandit groaned as I found his special spot and leaned into me. I. Loved. This. Dog.

"You and Bandit. He has never acted like that with anyone but me."

I glanced over my shoulder and saw Troy take off his hat and run his fingers through his hair. "Please, just for the night. If he drives you or me crazy, we can always drop him back off at your house." I knew Troy was going to say yes, and I knew Bandit wasn't going to be a problem this evening.

"Alright. Let me go grab his food and bowl," Troy said. He walked back into his house, mumbling under his breath.

"I think we are going to be great buddies," I cooed to Bandit.

Troy was back in a flash, now holding a plastic bag full of all of Bandit's doggie things and locked the front door.

"All right. Let's hit it. The food should be ready by now." I gingerly got up off the ground, careful of my ribs and made my way over to the truck. I opened the door, and Bandit leaped in and plopped his ass next to Troy. I hoisted myself up and slammed the door shut.

I turned to look at Troy and came face to face with Bandit's wet nose. "Remember, you asked for this mongrel to come along." I wiped my cheek off where Bandit's tongue had made a swipe across my face and laughed.

"I have a feeling asking Bandit to come along is going to be my best decision I've made all day," I said. I scratched him behind his ears, and he sprawled out, his head resting in my lap.

"We'll see about that."

--*-*-*-*-*-*-*-*-*-*-*-*

Chapter 5

TROY

Marley was passed out at the end of the couch with Bandit sprawled out on top of her, and I was looking over the destruction of her living room. Chinese takeout containers and soda cans littered her coffee table and the credits of *Pretty Woman* were rolling on the TV.

I had put up a fight to watch something different, but as soon as Marley pulled out the 'I got kidnapped today' card, I really couldn't argue with her. She definitely played dirty and to win.

Bandit's head raised, looking at me as I started picking up the empty containers. "Shh. Stay," I said as I raised my hand, letting Bandit know he shouldn't move. He laid his head back down, but his eyes remained open and alert as he watched me gather everything and head to the kitchen.

After I had dumped everything in the garbage, I glanced at the clock and saw that it was only nine o'clock and shook my head. Having worked second shift for close to ten years, nine o'clock at night was not even close to bed time for me. Opening the fridge, I saw she had beer and not much else to eat, which was fine because beer was what I was looking for.

Walking back into the living room, I dimmed the lights and headed out to the front porch. Bandit's eyes followed me the whole time, but he made no move to leave Marley's side. Leaving the door open, I quietly shut the screen door and took a seat in the rocking chair right next to the door.

I didn't expect Marley to wake up, but I wanted to be close by just in case. I took a long pull from my beer and wondered what the hell I was doing. Having tried the whole relationship thing in the past, things just didn't work out for me. I think the longest relationship I had ever been in had been just over six months. That relationship ended for the same reason all the others did: Meg.

I just didn't understand how no one believed that Meg and I were just friends. It always blew my mind when after telling these girls till I was blue in the face that Meg was just a friend. They would still give me an ultimatum of either Meg or them, or they would just leave because they didn't believe me. It was for the best that all those girls left. I didn't want to be with someone who didn't believe what I said, but I use to hold out hope that there would be one girl who would trust me and stick around. Right now I was zero and fifteen in the girlfriend department.

"Shouldn't you be in taking care of my daughter and not out here drinking?"

Son of a bitch. I should have known Gravel would make an appearance tonight. "She's sleeping."

Gravel walked to the foot of the porch steps but stopped there. "I don't like you being with my daughter."

Straight to the fucking point. "I'm not with your daughter. You insisted on her having someone stay the night, so she picked the one person she knew would piss you off. Here I am," I said, holding my arms out, wide.

Gravel shook his head and shoved his hands in his pockets. "Marley has enough shit going on in her life right now. She doesn't need you."

"You're acting like I insisted on being here, Gravel. I think you need to take a step back and take a look at things. Maybe figure out why your daughter would rather be with me, a guy she met twenty-four hours ago, instead of being with you, her father."

Gravel's face turned bright red, and I could see his rage. I took a long drink and waited for his response. I didn't want there to be a fight between Gravel and me, but he just kept coming at me, telling me to leave Marley alone, acting like I was the one pursuing her. I wasn't going to let him railroad over me.

"Our relationship has nothing to do with you. Stay away from her. She's got problems following her from California she needs to focus on right now, not some hick in cowboy boots."

"What do you mean problems following her?" I asked, ignoring his dig at my cowboy boots. It wasn't anything I hadn't heard before.

A grin spread across Gravel's face. The prick liked knowing something I didn't. "Well, I think I'll just head on back to Ethel's." He shoved his hands back in his pockets and headed back down the sidewalk.

"Don't you think I should know what kind of trouble Marley is in, seeing as I'm the only person she wants around her?" I called from the porch.

Gravel stopped in his tracks but didn't turn around. "I think that's a question you need to ask Marley, seeing as you're the only one she wants around and all." Gravel headed down the sidewalk and turned the direction of Ethel's. I watched him walk away until he faded into the darkness.

I tipped back the last of my beer and crushed the empty can with my hand. Marley was in trouble? More trouble than her being kidnapped by the Assassins? Although that had been cleared up by the fact, the idiots had thought she was Cyn.

What problem could have possibly followed Marley from California? She was a hairdresser for Christ's sake. How much trouble could she possibly get into?

--*-*-*-*-*-*-*-*-*-*-*

Chapter 6

Marley

I rolled over and came face to face with a wall of gray fur. I pushed away from Bandit and looked around. The last I remembered was falling asleep watching *Pretty Woman* on the couch, and now I was miraculously in my bed.

Bandit rolled over on his back, his legs pointing up to the ceiling and he cocked his head at me. His mouth was open with his tongue hanging out the side as he panted, anxiously waiting for me to pet him.

"You sure are a goofy boy," I cooed as I scratched his neck and ears.

As I was in the middle of Bandit's morning rub down, the door slowly swung open. "Bandit, come 'ere boy," Troy whispered as he walked into the room, but stopped in his tracks when he saw Bandit and me.

I pulled the comforter up around me, not knowing what I was wearing, but didn't stop petting Bandit.

"I didn't mean to wake you. I was just coming to try and pry Bandit away from you so he could go outside quick."

Bandit shot up from the bed at the mention of going outside. He jumped and whined on the bed excited to go outside.

"Stop," Troy ordered, holding his hand out like I had seen him do before. Bandit immediately sat down, but his tail still thudded against my leg, wagging.

"Did you start the coffee?" I asked as I peeked under the covers and saw I was still wearing the same clothes I had changed into when we had gotten home last night.

"First thing I did. I'll let you get dressed and meet you in the kitchen." Troy patted his leg, and Bandit jumped off the bed and was right on Troy's heels as they walked out the door and down the stairs.

I whipped the sheet back, sat up, and swung my legs over the side of the bed. I felt the side of my head, feeling the tender spot, thankful the pounding in my head had subsided.

Gingerly standing up, I felt my ribs moan in protest. Slowly stretching my arms over my head, I cursed Big A and his goons.

Running a brush through my hair, I looked over my appearance. It was definitely lacking. If I could take back Troy seeing me like this, I would be happy. My once silky blonde hair was plastered to one side of my head, and the other looked like Bandit had been licking it all night. I touched it, just to make sure it wasn't wet.

My face was makeup-free, which was how I typically looked unless I was doing something special other than going to work or lounging around the house. My eyes looked tired, and I had a crease from my pillow lined my face. I looked like a wreck, to put it mildly.

After fixing a nights worth of sleeping like the dead next to Bandit, I looked in the mirror and was much happier with what I saw. I grabbed a hair tie out of the pile I had on my nightstand and headed down the stairs as I twisted my hair up into a messy bun and followed my nose to the coffee.

Reaching up into the cabinet for my favorite cup, I heard Troy and Bandit ambling down the hallway to the kitchen.

I loved where I lived. It was almost what I had always dreamed up growing. Although growing up, my biggest wish was to not live an apartment anymore. When mom and I had lived with Gravel, we had also lived in an apartment, but it felt like home. After we had left, nothing felt like home.

Now my place in Rockton finally felt like home. It had a porch that spanned the front of the house that I loved to sit on and just watch the world go by. As you walked in the front door, you walked right into the living room, and the stairs to the upstairs were to the left. If you walked into the living room and down the hall, the half bath was on the right, and all the way down the hall was the kitchen. It was painted slate gray on three of the walls and a bright sunshine yellow on the fourth wall. I loved it. It was where I spent most of my time when I was at home even though I couldn't cook to save my life.

Holding the delicious cup of coffee up to my mouth I blew on it and watched Troy walk in the kitchen with Bandit, once again, right on his heels. Troy was wearing a dark navy blue tee and washed out jeans that were ripped at both knees. His tee was stretched taut across his shoulders, and it took all my willpower not to openly stare at him as he took his cup off the counter and refilled it.

"Thanks for making the coffee," I said, trying to distract myself from analyzing what color brown his eyes were as he looked at me.

"No problem. I was going to make breakfast, but I wasn't sure what you wanted."

"Oh, there's really not a lot to choose from. I'm not much of a cook, so breakfast is normally either cereal or a toaster pastry."

"I saw you had bacon and eggs. OK if I cook that up?" Troy asked, making his way to where I kept the pans I barely used and grabbed out my big fry pan.

"Um, if you want. Ethel went grocery shopping for me when I first got here. I forgot to tell her I wasn't much of a cook. She bought a bunch of stuff I can't make," I said, trying to explain my full freezer and why I ate cereal for breakfast.

"Cool, I wish my freezer was as stocked as yours is. I'm lucky if I have milk that isn't expired in my fridge." Troy grabbed the eggs from the fridge and cracked six into a bowl.

"I'll grab the bacon," I mumbled, trying to make myself useful.

"Can you stick it in the microwave for a couple of minutes to thaw it out?"

"Sure." I shoved it in the microwave and turned it on defrost. "So, how come if you can cook you don't have any food in your house?"

"Because I don't know how to cook for one person. The meals I always make end up enough to feed an army. Whenever I cook, it's normally something I make for work and then I can share it with Meg and Cyn." Troy explained as he dumped the eggs into the frying pan and turned the burner on.

"Don't you have to have the pan hot before you add the eggs?" I wasn't Martha Stewart, but I did know the basics of cooking, at least, I thought I did.

"Naw, you got to cook scrambled eggs low and slow. Meg taught me that. She can cook a leather shoe, and it would taste good. That chick has got the magic touch when it comes to baking or cooking."

"She cooked all the food for your party, right?" I asked, remembering the pulled pork that had melted in my mouth. It was divine. I had thought that Ethel had cooked it.

"Oh yeah. That was definitely Meg's pork. I told her the only way I would let her throw me a party is if she made the pork, tacos, and red velvet cake."

"Well, then you are definitely right, she really does have a way with food," I smiled.

"You want to set the table while I fry up the bacon?"

"Sure." I grabbed the plates and silverware and headed to the dining room and flipped on the light.

I had to dig through the last few boxes left in the dining room I had in the corner to find my placemats and make quick work of getting the table set. As I was setting the last fork in place, I smelt the bacon cooking and knew it was only a matter of time before it was time to eat.

"You want to make another pot of coffee? Breakfast should be ready in five minutes," Troy said as I walked back to the kitchen. His back was turned to me as he flipped the bacon.

"We drank a whole pot of coffee already?" I asked, amazed as I grabbed the empty pot and filled it with water.

"More like I drank a whole pot. Coffee is a necessity for me in the morning."

"I would say so seeing as I only had one cup," I laughed.

After I had the coffee set to brew, Troy was filling two plates with bacon and eggs, and we headed to the table.

"Placemats and everything," Troy chuckled as we sat down.

"Hey, you said to set the table. I very rarely get to use my placemats. Most mornings are me stumbling down the stairs and eating a quick bowl of cereal over the sink."

"Well, I guess one good thing about me being here is my cooking."

I took a bite of eggs and groaned. How in the hell did Troy make scrambled eggs taste like the best thing I had ever eaten. I watched him make them, noticing he really didn't do anything out of the norm, but his eggs were anything but the norm. They were out of this world. "Oh my god, these are seriously the best eggs I have ever tasted," I said around a mouthful of eggs."

"They're just eggs, Sunshine," Troy smirked.

"What did you call me?" I asked, my fork suspended in mid-air.

"Sunshine."

"Why?" I asked, curious.

"Your hair and your, well… everything." Troy shrugged his shoulders and tore his eyes away from me.

"My everything, huh?"

"Jesus Christ," Troy mumbled under his breath.

"Well, now I feel obligated to say something I like about you. Let's see," I mused as my gaze traveled over Troy's body.

"You don't need to say shit. Forget I ever called you Sunshine," Troy gruffed, grabbing his half empty plate and dumped it down the garbage disposal.

"No, no. I like it."

Troy just shook his head started making water to do the dishes.

"I like your shoulders," I blurted out as I watched his tee stretch taut across his shoulders.

"My shoulders, huh? Must be slim pickings of things you like about me if that was the only thing you could come up with," He laughed as he walked over to the table, grabbed his cup and filled it up.

I glanced at my cup, seeing I had only drunk half of it and wondered how the hell Troy could drink so much coffee and not be bouncing off the walls all the time. He leaned against the counter and crossed his legs in front of him, staring me down. "I think you telling me you like my shoulders is like me telling you I like your nose."

"What's wrong with my nose?" I raised my hand, trailing my fingertips down my nose, wondering if Troy thought it was big.

"There's nothing wrong with your nose, it goes perfectly with your face. I'm just saying telling someone you like their shoulders, isn't really a normal compliment."

"Well, I like them. They seem sturdy and well, can you know, shoulder stuff well." Shoulder stuff well, really Marley. Just shoot me now.

"Good use of shoulders, shouldering stuff," Troy smirked, taking a drink of his coffee.

"Yup, well, I think I'm just going to quit while I'm ahead." I glanced out the window looking into the backyard, praying Troy would let it go.

"So how does one actually measure how well they can shoulder things? Is there like a scale you go by? Do you walk down the street and think, 'Wow, he sure does have a set of shoulders on him.'?"

"You're an ass."

"I'm not an ass."

"Yes, you are. Total ass."

"Oh, so now we are talking asses. I'm partial to a good ass too. So you measure asses the same way you measure shoulders. Should I turn around?" Troy set his cup down turned around and braced his arms on the counter.

"I can't believe this is happening."

"Oh, it's happening alright. Do I need to shake it for you? Flex it? Or, is it all about the feel?" Troy stood up straight and reached around, squeezing his own ass.

I covered my eyes and burst out laughing. I couldn't watch any more.

"Holy shit. What the hell did I just walk into?"

I whipped my hands off my face, my eyes and saw Meg and Cyn standing in the doorway of the kitchen. Their eyes were glued to Troy, who still had his hands on his ass, but he was now looking over his shoulder at them.

"Marley likes my shoulders. I was trying to find out if she liked my ass before you two walked in. Ever hear of knocking?" Troy still had his hands on his ass. Was he going to stand like that all day?

"We did knock, no one answered. Dude, stop feeling yourself up," Meg replied, tearing her horrified gaze away from Troy and glanced at me.

I gave a little wave, unsure of what to say to someone who had just seen a guy groping himself, asking me if I liked his ass.

"I smell coffee." Cyn walked over to the coffee pot and held her hand out to Troy. He reached up in the cabinet and handed her a cup.

"Me too, cowboy," Meg ordered, holding her hand.

"I'm gonna have to make another pot with you two here."

"Please, even if we wouldn't have shown up, you would have made another pot. Coffee runs through your veins." Meg held her cup out to Cyn, who filled it up, and they both came to sit at the table with me.

"There's a dog under your table," Meg said, leaning over to glance under the table.

"It's Bandit," Troy said, his arms crossed over his chest.

"Holy shit, buddy. I didn't even know you were here!" Meg slid out of her chair and crawled under the table with Bandit.

After Troy and I had sat down to eat breakfast, Bandit had curled up by my feet and hadn't moved. His tail was wagging like crazy, beating against the leg of the table, but he had yet to move away from me.

"I should have brought Bluesy over if I had known you were here, handsome," Meg cooed from under the table.

"Um, does anyone what to tell her she's sitting under the table?" I asked, laughing.

"There's no point. She's weird," Cyn said, rolling her eyes.

"Hey, we're all fucking weird, I just don't care who sees my weird," Meg called.

"I don't think she could hide it if she wanted to," Troy chuckled.

"If I cared, I would so be offended by that," Meg said, crawling out from under the table and sat back in her chair.

"How come Bandit won't come out from under the table?" Cyn asked, glancing under the table.

Bandit had curled up by my feet again after his visit with Meg.

"He likes Marley. He hasn't left her side the whole time he's been here except to go outside and eat," Troy explained, filling his cup for the umpteenth time.

"Hmm, interesting," Meg said, her eyes darting back and forth between Troy and me.

"Knock it off, Meg," Troy said sternly.

"Never mind me," she purred, taking a sip of her coffee.

"Yeah, that's not likely. Why don't you spill on what the hell you two are doing here so early?"

"It's ten-thirty, Troy. Not exactly the butt crack of dawn," Cyn laughed.

"For you two it is." Troy shot Meg a look and shook his head.

"I was wondering what time you have to work today," Meg asked, turning her attention to me.

"She's not fucking working today!" Troy bellowed.

We all turned our gazes to Troy, who had pushed away from the counter and had a scowl on his face.

"You just got kidnapped twenty-four hours ago and have a concussion. You are not going to work." He crossed his arms over his chest and stared me down.

Ha! So Troy thought he was going to tell me what I was going to do. How cute.

"Dude, chill out. I'm pretty sure Marley can decide for herself what she's going to do. Right, Marley?" Meg scolded.

All eyes turned to me. "I don't think I'm going to work today," I replied.

"Ha! Told ya," Troy gloated.

"You're an ass," Meg pouted.

"But not because Troy said so, only because the salon is closed on Mondays," I said, bursting Troy's bubble.

"Yes!" Meg shouted, jumping up from her chair. "I knew it! Marley is one kick ass chick that you aren't going to be able to push around." Meg folded her arms over her chest and gave Troy an eat shit look.

"I'm not trying to push her around, I just want her to be careful."

"Sure. Whatever you say, cowboy," Meg said, rolling her eyes.

"These two could go at it all day if we let them," Cyn said, turning her attention back to me. "Meg and I came over wondering if you wanted to maybe go shopping or something. We all have to work at three, so it would just be a quick excursion."

Meg and Troy had ended their stare down and were waiting for my answer.

"Um, sure I guess. Is there anywhere to shop in town beside the grocery store, though?"

"We have to drive to Rivers Edge, which is like twenty minutes away," Cyn said as she grabbed our three empty cups and dumped them into the bubbly dishwater Troy had made.

"OK, just let me do the dishes and change and then we can head out."

"Nope. You go change and get ready, Cyn and I can do the dishes while we grill Troy about your night together." Meg elbowed me in the side as we stood up.

"I'd make a break for it now while you can," Cyn laughed.

"Um, I'll be right back," I mumbled walking out of the kitchen. Sprinting up the stairs, I glanced behind me when I heard Bandit galloping up the stairs after me.

I held my door open for Bandit to walk in and then slammed it shut and glanced around my room. Bandit leaped up on my bed and burrowed under the blankets. I wonder if Troy, Meg, and Cyn would notice if I just got under the covers with Bandit and didn't come back down.

Although they would probably send Troy up here to get me. Troy in my room was the last thing I wanted right now. Although I really had no idea what I wanted right now.

I closed my eyes and tried to focus on what was important right now. Whenever I would get overwhelmed, I would close my eyes and try to clear my head and let the most important thing that needed to be done come to the front.

After two minutes of clearing my mind, the only thing that came to the front and wouldn't go away was Troy.

Ha! Troy was definitely not the most important thing to focus on right now. Mark's family possibly finding me in Rockton that was important, not Troy. Troy was just a one night fling and would be nothing more. Except I hadn't planned on ever seeing Troy again. Troy wasn't supposed to be Troy. He was supposed to be some random guy who helped me forget my problems for one night. Which had totally worked until I had woken up in his bed and headed home only to be kidnapped and then find out Mr. Right Now was Troy.

Gah! Focus, Marley. Get dressed. That was the thing I needed to focus on right now. "Get dressed, on it," I said out loud as I made my way to my closet and slid the doors open.

I grabbed the first thing I saw and quickly changed out of my bed clothes. I took my hair down from the messy knot I had thrown it up in and quickly twisted it into a french braid. I bypassed makeup, just swiping on some lip balm and grabbed my purse by the door.

I whistled for Bandit to follow me and watched as he crawled to the foot of the bed under the blanket and peaked his nose out from the blanket.

"Come on, boy," I called, patting my leg.

Bandit leaped from the bed, taking the comforter with him, leaving it draped over his back like a cape. I laughed as I grabbed the blanket off his back and threw it back on the bed while Bandit waited by the door for me. "Let's go, handsome. I think today is going to be more interesting than either of us bargained for."

--*-*-*-*-*-*-*-*-*

Chapter 7

TROY

I was in hell. Shopping hell.

As the girls were getting ready to leave, Gravel's words popped into my head about Marley's problems following her from California, and I knew I couldn't let the girls go out by themselves.

So after Meg almost threw an all-out temper tantrum about me going with them, they finally all relented and let me come along.

Worst decision of my life. Ever.

After the twenty minute drive of constant talking from Meg and Cyn, and with Marley looking lost and confused, trying to keep up, I was ready to turn around and call it a day. I should have gone with that instinct.

"Do you think Rigid will like this top?" Cyn asked, walking out of the dressing with the same shirt she had shown me the past four times, just a different color each time. This time, it was orange, and it made her look like a pumpkin. Now came the hard decision of telling her the truth or lying.

"You look like a fucking gourd." Yep, my patience had gone from thin to non-existent.

"That's what I thought too," Cyn said, turning around to look at her ass in the huge mirror.

"Then take the fucking thing off. Why are you still looking at it?" I ask, irritated.

"Because it might be good for like a Halloween party, or when I make Rigid go pumpkin picking with me."

"Rigid pumpkin picking. I'd pay to see that shit. Although if you wear that top, a kid will be liable to pick you as his pumpkin."

"You're an ass," Cyn mumbled as she flipped me off and walked back into the dressing room.

I shook my head and leaned back in my chair and waited for the next train wreck of an outfit Meg or Cyn walked out in. Marley had yet to emerge from the dressing room. Maybe she was one of those chicks who didn't need to put on a fucking parade of all the clothes she was trying on.

Leaning my head against the wall, I closed my eyes and thought of anything but shopping.

"Shit, I thought Cyn was out here."

My eyes popped open at the sound of Marley's voice, and I leaned my head down.

Wow. Holy shit.

"Uh, she went back to the dressing room," I replied dumbly as I took in the short, black dress Marley had on. One hand was holding up the front, and the other was twisted behind her back.

"I'll go knock on her door." She walked backward and slammed into the wall. Her face heated red, and she ducked her head down and side-stepped to the left.

"Wait, just stop before you run into something else. Do you need help?"

"Um, yeah. I can't seem to get the zipper up on this."

"Turn around. I'll get it." I stood up, and Marley shuffled her way over to me and turned around.

I almost swallowed my tongue when I saw the back of the dress gaping open and her hand frantically trying to clutch it shut.

"I got it," I whispered, taking the one side of the dress out of her hand. I grabbed the other side of the dress and held them together with my left hand and my gaze traveled down her flawless back.

The zipper ran to the top of her ass and where I should have seen her underwear, all I saw was the crack of her ass. Fuck me, Marley wasn't wearing underwear.

My hand instinctively traced down the curve of her back, and I heard her breath hitch at the touch of my hand.

"Perfect skin," I mumbled, leaning down and placing a light kiss on her shoulder.

"Troy," she gasped at the touch of my lips but didn't pull away.

"Shh, I just had to remember what your skin felt like under my lips."

"We shouldn't be doing this," she whimpered as my right hand slid into the opening in the back and caressed her smooth skin.

"It's not anything we haven't done before," I whispered in between kisses across her shoulders.

"That was different then."

"How?" I growled as I felt her body relax into me.

"We didn't know each other. We were just two people looking for release. Now it's different." Her voice was breathy and airy.

"I think we're still both looking for that release. We both know what we can give each other. I want it again," I whispered in her ear and tugged on her lobe with my teeth.

"What happens after?"

"We sleep for a couple of hours and then I take you again and again." I let go of her dress and pull her sweet, lush body to mine. I had never been more turned on in all of my life as I had been standing in that dressing room. I needed to have Marley again.

"No one can know, please." She tilted her head to the left, giving me access to kiss her neck.

"Ashamed of me, Sunshine?" I teased.

"No, I just don't need to deal with my dad when it comes to you. He wouldn't understand. He only sees things in black and white."

"So we'll just be each other's release?" I growled as she thrust her ass into my dick.

"Like a trigger."

"OK, go get dressed. We'll continue this tonight when I get off of work." I slowly slid my hand out of her dress, missing her touch as soon as she stepped away from me.

"You still need to do up the back of my dress," she said, her back still turned to me, the dress wide open in the back.

"Right. Sorry," I mumbled, stepping forward and pulling the zipper up.

"Thanks," she whispered and ran back into her dressing room.

I sat back down, my dick protesting every move and stretched my legs out in front of me.

What the hell did I just agree to? We both knew that we weren't what we needed, but damned if we both didn't want it.

I reclined my head back and tried to calm my dick by counting backward from 100. By the time, I hit forty-three I had things under control. I kept my eyes shut and tried to think of anything besides Marley.

"Wow, those dressing room walls sure are thin," Meg said in my ear right before she dumped a pile of clothes in my lap.

"Jesus Christ, do I look like a fucking hamper to you?" I pushed the clothes off my lap and onto the chair next to me.

"I thought you might have to carry my stuff to hide the major boner you probably have right now." She smirked and propped her hands on her hips.

"You didn't hear anything, Meg. I mean it." I stood up, face to face with her.

"Oh, you mean I didn't hear you two make plans to pick up where you left off tonight?"

"Yes. She doesn't want anyone to know." I crossed my arms over my chest and prayed Meg would keep her mouth shut.

"I won't say a word. Although it might be kind of hard to see Marley tonight seeing as Lo had put a guy on her at all times from the club. I won't say anything, but I really doubt Hammer will keep his mouth shut when he sees you sneak into Marley's house tonight." Meg mimicked me, crossing her arms over her chest.

"Tell King she doesn't need protection. The Assassins aren't going to come after her again."

"He's not worried about the Assassins, Marley has other problems that, unfortunately, neither of us know about."

"Then I'll be her fucking bodyguard."

"You have work, and how would you explain that to Gravel?"

"This is bullshit. I'm never gonna be able to see her if someone from the club is always going to be with her." I took my hat off and ran my fingers through my hair. Son of a bitch.

"I have an idea, but you're going to have to keep it in your pants until the weekend," Meg said, rubbing her hands together.

I knew the look she had on her face. I had seen it many times before when she was cooking up some scheme in her head. This was going to be a fifty/fifty shot at working out. I just had to decide if I was willing to hedge all on my money on Meg's harebrained idea.

"What's happening this weekend?" Cyn asked walking out of the dressing room with her own mountain of clothes in her arms.

"Operation Snake in the Grass."

"What?" Cyn and I asked at the same time.

"Alright, alright. I need to think of a new name. Operation Panty Raid?"

"Are we going to act like thirteen-year-old boys and raid the cheerleader's panty drawers?" Cyn asked, even more, confused now.

"What?! No. Do you two have no imagination at all?" Meg threw her hands up in the air, annoyed with Cyn and me.

"Dude, I have no idea what you are talking about. Just spit it out with all this code name shit," Cyn said as she threw her pile of discarded clothes on top of Meg's.

"Troy and Marley want to hook up, but they don't want the club knowing, specifically Gravel. That's where you and I come in and create a diversion," Meg explained.

"Was that so hard to say? All this cloak and dagger shit makes you even loonier than you normally are. I'm gonna go pay," Cyn said, grabbing two shirts off the top of the pile and headed to the checkout.

"Geez, she has to be PMSing." Meg shook her head as she watched Cyn walk away.

"Shut up, Meg. I'm gonna go see if Marley is done. We need to head back if we are going to make it back in time for work."

"Don't do anything I wouldn't do," Meg called as I made my way to Marley. I threw my hand up in the air but didn't say anything. Sometimes with Meg, you just needed to let her be herself and let her say whatever she wanted. It was easier that way.

There were four stalls for changing and only one had the door shut. I knocked on the door and prayed for Marley to be naked when she opened the door.

--*-*-*-*-*-*-*-*-*-*

Marley

"Just a sec," I called as I pulled my shirt over my head. After I finally got my heart beating at a normal pace, I had decided just to get the black dress and nothing else. Money was tight, and I didn't need to be blowing all my tips on clothes. If I really thought about it, I didn't need the black dress either, but I have plans to make this dress worth every penny when Troy came over.

I grabbed all my discarded clothes and made quick work of hanging them all back on the hangers and opened the door to see Troy standing there.

"Hi," I gulped out, surprised to see him.

"Meg and Cyn are paying and then we need to head back." I looked Troy up and down and saw no evidence of our encounter having any effect on him. When I had walked back into the dressing room and looked at myself in the mirror, my cheeks were stained red, and my pulse was beating a mile a minute. I had a split second thought of pulling Troy into the dressing room with me and see if he really wasn't affected or just a good actor.

"Let's go! I wanna hit the pretzel place before we leave. Hustle!" Meg called.

There goes that idea. "I'll just hang these up and then check out. Five minutes tops, promise," I said, trying to sneak past Troy, who was standing right in my way.

"Go hang those up and I'll hold onto this for you." Troy grabbed the dress I had draped over my arm and headed out of the dressing room without a backward glance.

I made quick work of hanging up all the clothes I didn't want and looked around for Troy, but couldn't find him. I headed to the front of the store and saw him standing with Meg and Cyn waiting for me.

"Where's the dress?"

"Right here," Troy said, handing me a plastic shopping bag.

"You bought my dress?" I asked dumbly as I grabbed the bag from him and looked inside. Yup, sure as shit, there was the dress laying folded inside.

"Yeah. Let's go. Meg's hungry and when she doesn't eat, she gets hangry." Troy grabbed the bag out of my hand and headed for the exit.

"Stop. You can't buy me clothes."

"I can, and I did." Troy grabbed my hand and tried pulling me to the door. I dug my heels in and refused to budge.

"No. Take it back or let me pay you," I insisted.

"Oh, how cute. Rigid and I had this same fight over groceries," Cyn said, looking all sappy as she watched Troy try to pull me out of the store.

"And then remember the motorcycle boots he insisted on buying for you. You attempted to fight him, but in the end, he won," Meg added.

"Yup. I can't remember King ever insisting on buying you something, though." Cyn crossed her arms, thinking.

"That's because every time he says he'll pay, I let him pay. That's something you two need to learn. If he says he'll pay, go with it," Meg said, staring me down.

"That's because King is your boyfriend. Troy is just, well, Troy," I sputtered.

"Yup, that's right, I'm Troy. Let's go. You can pay me back later for the dress," Troy said as he tugged one last time on my arm and I gave in.

"Just let me give you the money now," I insisted.

"It's not money you're going to pay me back with."

"Oh, now this sounds good," Meg said to Cyn as we walked out of the store and towards the pretzel place.

"Troy, I thought no one was going to know," I said worriedly glancing behind us.

"They're gonna help us. Don't worry. Their alliance is to me, not Gravel," Troy said, trying to reassure me.

I didn't say anything more because I guess he was right in a sense, but who's to say King or Rigid wouldn't find out and tell Gravel. I might have just agreed to be Troy's hook up without really thinking about it. Shit.

--*-*-*-*-*-*-*-*-*-*

Chapter 8

Marley

"Bandit!" I called into the backyard. Troy had dropped me off at my house after grabbing pretzels at the mall and said he would be back after work to pick up Bandit after I insisted he stay with me while Troy worked. There was no sense in Troy taking Bandit home when he could stay with me.

It was past eleven o'clock, and I was basically on pins and needles waiting for Troy to get off work and come over. I was going to wear the dress tonight, but I had decided against thinking it would look like I was trying too hard so I had settled on my cute, but sexy pajamas.

I heard a motorcycle roar by and rolled my eyes. Every hour, on the hour, someone from the club would drive by, checking up on me. Ridiculous.

I had called Gravel the third time I had heard and seen them drive by, but Gravel insisted it was for my own protection. I had no idea if they were going to continue their drive-bys through the night or not. It looked like the night I had planned with Troy might not go the way we had hoped.

Hearing a truck pull in the driveway, Bandit bolted past me, around the house headed for Troy. Bandit may have liked staying with me, but I could tell he had missed Troy.

As I rounded the house, I saw Troy's truck door open, and only Bandit's back legs.

"Down boy. I'm happy to see you too," Troy said as he climbed out of the truck.

"He missed you," I said walking up to him.

"He just knows I'm the one who feeds him." Troy kneeled next to Bandit and rubbed him behind his ears, and he groaned in appreciation.

"Our plans might have a slight hitch in them tonight."

"I know. Meg told me after she talked to King that they had prospects drive by your house to make sure everything looked OK," Troy said, standing up and brushing his pants off.

"Yup, like clockwork. They just drove by not even five minutes ago."

"So every hour they drive by?" Troy asked, stepping closer to me.

"Yeah."

"So that means we're good for an hour?"

"Give or take."

"Not as much time as I'd like, but it does for now." Troy took one step closer and wrapped his arms around me.

"Don't tell me we're going for an eight-second ride, cowboy," I said, grabbing Troy's baseball hat off his head and plopping it on my head backward.

"Oh no, Sunshine. I'm gonna take you for a ride, but it's gonna be much longer than eight seconds."

"Yeehaw," I whispered right before Troy's lips crashed down on mine. He spun me around, our lips still connected and leaned me against the side of his truck.

"You taste better each time I kiss you," he growled against my lips. I glided my hands up his arms and delved my fingers in his hair, gripping his head. Troy's kisses were like a drug I couldn't get enough of. Every time our lips touched I yearned for more.

Bandit started crying and pawing at my leg. "Bandit's jealous," I said in between kisses.

"Bandit had you all night to himself, it's my turn now."

"Think you're both jealous of each other," I laughed, tilting my head to the side as Troy rained kisses down my neck.

"If you would-" Bandit started going crazy barking and standing on his hind legs, trying to get in between Troy and me.

"I think there's something wrong with him, Troy,"

"Yeah, he's not the center of attention. Down, Bandit," Troy ordered, holding his hand up. Bandit bit down on Troy's sleeve and yanked his arm down.

"Troy, I think we-," Gunfire blasted through the quiet night, and Troy tackled me to the ground and grabbed Bandit.

Three more gunshots rang out and then tires squealed as the car took off.

"Stay here," Troy ordered and then army crawled to the back of the truck. He got up on his knees and peeked behind the truck.

Bandit's wet nose nudge my hand, and I jumped, scared. I wrapped my arm around his neck and cuddled him close to me. Troy and I had just been shot at. Holy fuck.

"Call King, although I'm sure with that much gunfire, someone already called the cops, and I'm sure Gravel is running down the road right now. Stay. Here." Troy glanced back at me.

I nodded my head, letting him know I wasn't going anywhere and then he disappeared behind the truck.

Bandit whined in my arms and rested his head on my leg.

"Where the hell is Marley?" I heard Gravel bellow at Troy.

I knew I should get up or at the very least say something, but I couldn't. I was paralyzed.

"She's behind the truck with Bandit. She's okay," Troy hollered back.

"Good, now tell me what the hell happened. I called King as soon as I heard the first shot, he should be here any minute."

I lifted my hand to pet Bandit's head, and I saw my handshake, but it was like I couldn't even feel them. My heart was beating a mile a minute, and my breathing was short and shallow.

"Troy," I shakily called. I had to get a grip, but I had no idea how to. We were just shot at. Someone just tried to kill Troy and I. "Troy!" I screamed, losing it.

"I thought you said she was fine!" I heard Gravel yell as I wildly whipped my head back and forth looking for Troy.

Bandit whined again in my arms and rested his paw on my arm. Jesus Christ, even the dog was trying to comfort me.

Troy and Gravel ran around the side of the truck. Troy dropped to his knees next to me and cradled my head in his hands. "Shh, Sunshine, you're fine," Troy murmured.

"Someone just shot at us, Troy," I said dumbly like Troy wasn't there.

"I know. We're OK, though. So is Bandit. Nothing to worry about." Troy stroked my cheek with his thumb, wiping away the tears I didn't even know I was crying.

"No, we're not! Someone tried to kill us!" I shrieked, my panic going into overdrive.

"Shh, look at me, Marley." I shook my head no, unable to calm down. "Marley, look at me right now," Troy demanded, his voice stern.

My eyes whipped to his, and a cry escaped my lips.

"You're OK. Don't worry, Sunshine. Gravel's here, and King and the rest of the guys will be here any minute. They'll take care of everything. I promise."

"You can't promise everything will be OK, Troy. You don't know that. Mark's family is here, and they just tried to kill us. Nothing is OK with that," I whispered.

Troy wrapped his arms around me and pulled me close. I had never felt more scared but so safe. "I promise, Marley. With everything I have, nothing is going to happen to you."

"Take her into the house. Ethel is on the way over. She'll sit with her while we figure out what the hell is going on," Gravel said as he shoved his phone in his pocket.

I clung to Troy, not wanting him to let me go. "Stand up, Sunshine. Let's get you in the house and not sitting on the ground." Troy patted my back, and I pushed away from him. He brushed my hair out of my face and gave me a swift kiss on the forehead before he stood up and held his hand out to me.

I grabbed his hand, and he hoisted me up, sliding his arm around my waist. "I'm sorry," I whispered as we walked up the porch steps.

"Nothing to be sorry about. Being shot at isn't something someone should be able to brush off like it's nothing."

Opening the front door, Bandit bounded in ahead of us, and Troy's hand slipped from my waist to the small of my back as he guided me into the living room towards the couch.

"Do you want me to stay with you until Ethel gets here?" Troy asked as I sat down on the edge of the sofa. I patted the cushion beside me and Bandit hopped up, plopping his butt down.

I heard the roar of motorcycles come down the street and pull into the driveway. The cavalry had arrived. "You should go outside and let everyone know what happened. I'll be okay until Ethel gets here." I tried sounding like I was OK, but I knew that I was one breath away from having a breakdown.

I heard a car door slam and knew that Ethel was here. Thank God. I didn't want to be a blubbering mess in front of Troy. I already looked like I had a screw loose when I lost it outside.

"She's here. You can head outside." I looked up at Troy whose gaze was trained on me.

"I'll come back in as soon as I can, OK?"

"OK," I whispered, nodding my head.

"Marley," Ethel called as she walked in the front door.

Bandit's ears perked up, and he leaned into me, trying to see past Troy, who was standing in front of me. "Hey, Ethel," I called.

"How are you holding up, sweetheart?"

"Oh, you know. Just a little ruckus."

Ethel threw her head back and laughed. "I knew you were a fighter."

"I'll be back. Take care of her for me, Ethel," Troy said as he slipped out the front door.

"Don't even have to ask, Troy. I'm here, and Meg is outside with Lo right now. Tell her to head on in and I'll whip up some hot chocolate," Ethel said as she pulled off her coat and draped it over the back of the recliner.

"Will do," Troy shut the door behind him, and Ethel turned to look at me.

"I think he's gone, sweetheart. You can stop clasping your hands together so tight. Your knuckles are turning white, dear." Ethel slipped her shoes off and walked over to me.

I looked down at my hands seeing that they were turning white. Unclasping them, I laid them on my knees and looked up at Ethel. "I'm pretty sure I'm going to lose it."

"Let it out, hun. No shame in it. I've thankfully never been shot at before, so I can't tell you how to feel."

"Hey!" Meg yelled, poking her head in through the front door.

"He told you about the hot chocolate, I take it?" Ethel laughed.

"Uh, duh. He didn't even have to finish his sentence before I was up the front steps. Need some help?" Meg walked in, shrugging her coat off and put it on top of Ethel's.

"I got it. Why don't you sit with Marley?"

"Can do," Meg said, saluting Ethel. Ethel walked down the hall to the kitchen, shaking her head and chuckling at Meg.

"How ya hanging in there?" Meg plopped down on the other side of Bandit, and he laid his paw on her knee and nudged her hand with his nose.

"Um, you know…" I watched Meg's hand as she patted Bandit, trying not to think about anything. When I started thinking about the fact I almost got shot, I started to lose my shit.

"You know Gravel got shot, right?" Meg leaned forward and pulled the coffee table closer to the couch and kicked her feet up.

"Yeah. He filled me in."

"Well, I was there. So was Cyn. I'm not sure how Cyn handled it, but I can tell you for the next month after it had happened, I was so damn jumpy and attached to Lo. It got better, though." Her gaze landed on me, and I could feel the compassion in her tone.

"I almost died," I whispered. Meg nodded her head and clasped my hand. "Troy almost died because of me." A lone tear ran down my cheek and dropped on my leg.

"It's not your fault. You didn't ask for those assholes to come and shoot at you."

"I need to leave. I shouldn't have come here. There's no reason why you guys should be in danger because of me, you barely know me. I'm leaving." I pushed away from the coffee table and stood up. I frantically looked around, trying to figure out where to start first.

"Ethel!" Meg called, but I ignored her. I decided packing my closet was the best place to start. Even though I had just bought furniture and everything I would have to leave it all behind again. I had no idea where I was going to go, but I knew I had to leave Rockton before anyone got hurt because of me.

I bounded up the stairs and threw open my bedroom door. Whipping open the closet door, I thanked God that I was such a procrastinator, and my empty cardboard boxes still sat on the floor. I tossed them out into the open and grabbed a handful of clothes and started ripping them off the hangers.

As I was grabbing the third handful of clothes, I heard yelling and talking coming from downstairs but couldn't make out what they were saying. I'm sure they were all grateful that I was leaving, even though I'm sure they'll protest me leaving.

"You packing up all your shit and leaving wasn't part of our deal."

I glanced up from my frantic packing and saw Troy leaning on the door frame.

"Neither was us getting shot at."

"You're not leaving, Marley. I'm not going to let you run away, and I can damn sure bet you that your dad isn't going to let you go. You need to let us help you."

"No. This is my mess, and I need to figure out how to fix it. I'm going back to California, and I'm going to talk to Mark's family. There has to be a way that I can make this better." I grabbed three pairs of shoes and tossed them on top of the overflowing box. "Tape. I need tape," I babbled. "Tape fixes everything."

"Marley! Stop!" Troy yelled.

"I need another box." There was no way I could stop. I was beyond frantic and headed into crazed.

I pushed the overflowing box out of the way and made my way back over to the closet.

"Marley, stop." Troy wrapped his arms around me from behind, stopping me in my tracks. "You need to take a breath and just relax."

"We almost died, Troy," I whispered.

"I know, but we didn't. We're both still here, having this ridiculous conversation." He tightened his arms around me and pulled my back flush to his front.

"It's not ridiculous. I don't want you to get hurt because of me. It's best if I just go."

"So you leave and then they can kill you? Sorry, not happening."

"You don't know what you are getting into, Troy. Hell, I don't even know what we are dealing with. I never thought that Mark's family would do something like that to me. I know they don't like me, but I never imagined they would try to kill me." I tilted my head back, resting it on Troy's shoulder.

"You're not leaving, Marley. It's not safe."

"No shit, Troy. That's why I'm leaving in the morning." I turned around in his arms and tilted my head back to look at him.

"You have to work. You just going to up and leave with no notice at your job?"

Shit, he was right. I couldn't leave Gwen with not even a days' notice. She had just started taking on more clients and was thinking of adding another stylist. "Dammit. You're right."

"I know," Troy smirked.

"So, I give my two weeks' notice and then I leave."

"How long was the lease you signed on this place?"

Son of a bitch. "One year."

"You think you can just walk out on poor, old Mrs. Petersen, leaving her high and dry with no one to rent this place to."

"How the hell do you know who I rent this place from?"

"Small town, Sunshine. You'll see once you stay for a while." His hand stroking my back.

"Nice try, but I'm not going to stay here long enough to see how it is living in a small town. Two weeks and I'm gone." I pushed away from Troy, trying to get away from his touch. He was making me lose focus on why I was leaving.

"Alright, two weeks. Not a day sooner. Deal?" Troy held his hand out for me to shake.

"Why do I feel like you agreeing with me leaving in two weeks so easily isn't as big of a victory as I think?" I asked, crossing my arms over my chest.

"Because it's not. You still have to deal with your dad. I figure between the two of us, there's no way you'll be leaving in two weeks."

Dammit. How the hell had I forgotten about Gravel? Troy was right, there was no way Gravel was going to let me leave if Mark's family was out there still trying to hurt me. I would have to try everything I could think of to get them to lay off. "I'll have everything cleared up in two weeks, and then I'm gone."

"If you get everything cleared up in two weeks, then why are you going to leave, Marley?" Troy asked, pulling me into his arms again.

"Because there's nothing here for me," I stared over Troy's shoulder, looking at the wall.

"That's bullshit. There's more here than there was in California. Your dad and everybody downstairs want you to stay."

"I can come and visit Gravel and everyone else. There's nothing here that can make me stay."

"What about me?"

My eyes snapped to Troy's. "What do you mean, what about you? Last I knew, Troy, we had agreed to casually hook up. I don't think a casual hook up is something that can tie me down."

"Maybe if you would stay and not run away, it could be something more. But with you insisting on leaving, that's all it's going to be."

I pushed on his chest and stepped out of his arms. "You said you only wanted casual before any of this happened so don't stand there and tell me you thought we could be something more all along. That's a lie."

Troy ran his fingers through his hair and looked up at the ceiling. "Jesus Christ, Marley. How the hell did we end up here, having this conversation?"

"I'm pretty sure it's cause you opened your big mouth." I crossed my arms over my chest and stared him down.

"I'm not doing this, Marley. This is the exact reason I don't want to be in a relationship. Fighting with you when you are irrational and twisting my words is not something I want."

"I didn't ask you to do this, Troy. You were the one who came on to me at the store, not me. If my irrational moods are too much for you to handle, I can show you where the door is," I ranted.

"I'm done. A half an hour ago we were ready to rip each other's clothes off, and now all we want to do is rip each other's heads off. All I want is for you to be safe and you can't see that. Leave or stay, Marley, it's up to you."

"Two weeks, I'm gone."

"Ok, well, I'll just say goodbye now."

"We're going to see each other before I leave, Troy. There's no need to be dramatic."

"That's where you're wrong, Marley." He walked towards me and reached out, cupping my cheek with his hand. "I wish you wouldn't leave, but I can't stop you. Please be careful." He leaned down and pressed a kiss to my forehead and walked out the door.

Bandit whined next to me and nudged my hand with his nose. I glanced down at him and rubbed his nose.

"Bandit!" Troy yelled up the stairs. Bandit whined again and nudged my leg.

I crouched down eye to eye with Bandit and cradled his head in my hands. "You need to go, boy. Troy is waiting for you."

Troy called for Bandit again, this time, there was no fooling around in his tone. Bandit walked to the door and looked back at me. I fell down on my knees and motioned for him to leave. He gave me one last glance and then disappeared down the hall, and I heard him pad down the stairs.

How did things change so quickly? An hour ago I had felt the happiest I had been in years. Now, I was sitting on the floor, my heart, even more, broke then when Mark had died.

Troy and I hadn't even dated, but it felt like I was losing a part of me I couldn't live without. It was probably for the best that we didn't see each other anymore, but it still fucking hurt.

Tears ran down my cheeks, spilling onto the floor. I couldn't see it before, but I might have let the best thing that could have happened to me walk out the door.

It was time to leave Rockton. Two weeks and all of this would be a memory.

--*-*-*-*-*-*-*-*-*

Chapter 9

TROY

"Troy!" I heard Meg call after me as I walked out the door with Bandit on my heels. I wasn't in the mood for whatever Meg had to say, so I kept walking.

"Son of a bitch, stop, you asshole!" Meg jerked on my arm right before I reached my truck and tugged on me to stop.

"Why the hell are you leaving?"

"Trust me, it's not my choice. Now, let go of my arm."

"No, not until you tell me what the hell changed in the past ten minutes. I knew the second you walked down the stairs something was wrong. Tell me," Meg insisted.

This was the problem with my friendship with Meg, we couldn't hide anything from each other. Even when neither of us talked, we still knew what the other was thinking. "Marley is leaving."

"What?"

"Two weeks. She's giving notice at work and then she's gone."

"Why the hell would she do that? She just rented this house and bought all sorts of shit. That doesn't make sense."

"She's trying to protect us by leaving." I reached up and ran my fingers through my hair.

"So she leaves and the douche canoes that attempted to kill her tonight find her fifty miles down the road. It's not safe for her to leave. She needs to stay and let the club help her."

"Fuck, Meg. I know that. What the hell did you think I was doing up there. She wouldn't listen to me."

"So you're just going to leave her."

"Meg, I can't do this. She doesn't want me, I'm not going to hang around hoping she'll come around and decide to stay. She made her decision, so now I made mine." I opened up the driver's door and slipped into the truck.

Meg grabbed the door before I could shut it and held it open. "She made the wrong decision, Troy. She's going to see that. You know Gravel isn't going to let her leave."

"Look, Meg. Marley and I had one night together. We've barely known each other for twenty-four hours. I can't expect her to listen to me and decide for her. We're not meant for more than one night."

"That's shit, Troy. You want more, I can see it."

"Hell yeah I want to spend more time with her, but not with her leaving. I'm getting too old to play all of these fucking games. She's dead set on leaving, and I told her I want her to stay. She doesn't care. That's all I can do."

"Maybe if you hang out with her these next two weeks she'll stay."

"No. I told her if she was leaving she wouldn't see me again, and I meant it. Tonight was the last time I'll see Marley. It's best this way Meg, and I'd appreciate it if you'd back me on this and not try to convince me otherwise."

"I'm your best friend, Troy. You know I'll back you on anything. I just wish you would think about this some more before you write off Marley. She's scared right now and not thinking clearly."

I stuck the key in the ignition and cranked the truck up. I pressed the button to roll the window down and grabbed the door out of Meg's hold and slammed it shut. "I'm not playing games and sitting around waiting for Marley to change her mind."

Meg leaned against the truck, sticking her head through the window. "Go home and sleep on it. I think you're both making a mistake."

"Look, Meg. I appreciate what you are trying to do here, but I really don't think things are going to change. Just make sure King has someone watching Marley." I shifted the truck into gear and waited for Meg to step away from the truck.

"You're really not going to come around, are you?" Meg said. I think it was finally sinking in that I wasn't going to hang around and try to convince Marley to stay.

"No. I'll see you at work." She stared at me, nodded her head and backed away from the truck.

I backed down the driveway and headed back to my house. Bandit whined next to me and watched Marley's house disappear behind us. "It's OK boy." I reached over and scratched his ears. He leaned his head into my hand and gave the most pathetic whine I had ever heard.

I didn't know what to do. Leaving Marley was not something I wanted to do, but she was going to leave in two weeks anyway. I know she was being irrational and not thinking things through, but dammit, she wouldn't even listen to reason. I understood she didn't want any of us to get hurt, but running away was not the solution.

I had seen how the Devil's Knights handle problems, and I had no doubt that they would be able to help Marley and take care of her situation. Why she couldn't see that and thought the only way to solve it was to leave was beyond me.

Maybe Gravel was right. Marley's kind of problems and trouble weren't what I wanted. As of right now, I was better off alone.

--*-*-*-*-*-*-*-*-*

Chapter 10
Marley

"God dammit, Marley. Get that fucking nonsense of leaving out of your head. If I have to tie you to a chair, I damn well will," Gravel fumed at me as he paced in front of the couch I was sitting on.

It was two days after the whole shooting and Troy leaving disaster. Ethel and Gravel had been staying with me since, and I was two seconds away from saying fuck it and not work out my two weeks' notice I had promised Gwen.

Gravel was driving me insane. If he wasn't ranting at me about not leaving, he was outside patrolling the house, making sure no one would be able to get in.

"Lincoln, sit down before you have a heart attack. You ranting at Marley isn't going to make her stay. Hell, I want to leave, and you're not even talking to me." Ethel walked into the living room and sat in the recliner next to the couch.

"I can't calm down when my daughter who I haven't seen in years finally comes to town, and now she's fucking leaving while her ex's douche lords family is trying to kill her." Gravel ran his fingers through his hair, pulling out the tie he had holding it back.

"You need a haircut." Yup, totally trying to distract Gravel. I had been attempting to talk him into cutting his hair since I had came into town and it pissed him off each time I suggested it.

"I'll get a goddamn haircut if you agree to stay." Gravel crossed his arms over his chest and stared me down.

Why didn't anyone understand I was leaving to keep them safe? I planned on going back to California and facing Mark's family to get everything figured out. After that, I had no idea where I was going to go. I knew I wasn't going to stay in California. My mother and a handful of friends were the only things I had left there. I had always wanted to travel and see all fifty states, but I would have to win the lotto to make that a possibility.

"Why can't you hear what I'm saying? I need to go talk to Mark's family and fix everything." I grabbed the pillow from the end of the couch and hugged it to my chest.

"Because they are past the point of talking, Marley! Anyone can see that. If they wanted to speak to you, they wouldn't have sent someone to come and kill you for Christ sakes!" Gravel yelled.

"Lincoln, go outside and calm down. Let me talk to Marley without you ranting." Ethel raised her arm and pointed to the front door.

"You're not going to be able to talk sense to her any more than I am," Gravel mumbled as he walked out the front door, the screen door slapping shut behind his retreating back.

"Your father is going about you leaving the wrong way, but he is right, hun. It's not safe for you to leave." Ethel popped open the footrest on the chair and reclined back.

"It's not safe for me to stay either."

"It's a lot safer than you think. Who's going to stay and protect you when you leave? Your plan is to go to California, but who's to say they won't kill you before you get there. Your reason for wanting to leave is honorable, but it's also stupid."

I leaned my head back and stared up at the ceiling. Was Ethel right? I hadn't thought about the fact that they might hurt me before I got to California. "I couldn't live with myself if someone got hurt because of this, Ethel. I don't know what to do. I left because I thought that would help make things better. I was wrong."

"Then the only way to make it right is to stay. You didn't know what was following you when you left California, this isn't your fault. Money makes people do crazy and violent things sometimes."

"Why didn't Gravel explain it to me like you just did?"

"Because that's not Gravel's way. He's a man who knows when he's right and what he wants. When things don't go the way he planned or wants, he yells. You have to know when to step back and really try to listen to what he is saying when he's yelling. What I just said was what Gravel was trying to tell you."

I glanced over and saw Ethel looking at me. "I'll stay, for now. If things get dangerous, though, I'll leave. Even without a two-week notice to work."

"Good, hun. You made the right choice. If after all of this blows over and you still want to leave, I promise to hold Gravel back," she winked at me.

"OK. I'm good with that." I kicked my feet up on the coffee table and stretched out my legs. I was wearing my favorite wore out lounge pants and a baggy sweatshirt. I had just gotten off of work and changed when Gravel had started in on me again about leaving. I'm sure once I told him I planned on not leaving, he would assume it was because of his nagging.

"That's it. I can't deal with this," Gravel shouted, walking through the front door, "you are staying, and I don't give two shits if you don't like it. I'm your father, and I'm just trying to protect you." He stopped in front of the couch and stared me down.

I glanced over at Ethel, who was smirking at me. I winked at her and turned my attention back to Gravel. "OK."

"Thank fucking God!" he shouted and threw his arms up in the air.

"But, I have two conditions."

"If it means you are staying, let's hear them." He crossed his arms over his chest and waited.

"One, I get to cut your hair. Now," I said, holding up one finger. His hair was driving me insane and was in dire need of a cut.

"Fine. Ethel and I talked about you cutting it when you first came in, so now is as good as time as any."

"Two, you and Ethel need to leave. If you insist on having someone here with me, I get to choose who it is." I tossed the pillow at the end of the couch and stood up. This was the condition I knew Gravel was going to have a hard time with.

"No."

"Then I leave."

Gravel's phone blared from his pocket, interrupting our stare down. "Hold on, this isn't over," he mumbled to me as he pulled his phone out of his pocket and swiped left to answer it. He barked hello into it and walked back out the front door.

"You're not going to tell him you decided to stay before he came back in, are you?" Ethel laughed.

"Hell no. I might as well get something out of all the yelling and screaming he has been doing this past couple of days."

"Who are you going to have come stay with you?" Ethel asked.

"I'm not staying here, I'm going there." I had messed up with Troy. I had pushed him away when he was just trying to help me. I didn't know how I could miss someone so much after only knowing them for such a short time. I guess this was what all those romance novels I read talked about. Insta-love. Although Troy and I were far from love. So, maybe insta-infatuation? Whatever the hell it was, I wanted to find out what it was. Troy was so much different from the men I had known growing up and who I had dated.

Mark was a businessman who left the house every morning in a suit and tie and very rarely had a spec of dirt on him. Troy, I hate to say it, but he was all man. The few times I had seen him, he was either wearing cowboy boots or work boots, and it seemed jeans and a tee were his standard attire, whether it was work or not.

"I never imagined you and Troy together," Ethel mused.

"He's definitely not the type of guy I used to find attractive. I'll have to see if he'll even let me in his house. The last time we talked, we didn't exactly leave things friendly." I sat back down on the couch, tucking my legs underneath me.

"Just talk to him, hun. I don't know Troy as well as I should, but he seems like a good man. Straight to the point, no nonsense."

"Yup, that is definitely the vibe I got off of him also. Plus he told me he's not into playing games." Gravel stomped back in the room and tossed his phone onto the coffee table.

"Pack your shit, you need to stay at the clubhouse until we clear up the shit storm that followed you. Things are not looking good right now." Gravel barked.

"Wait, what are you talking about?" What the hell had changed from the time Gravel's phone rang to now?

"Mark's family has direct dealings with the Banachi family. His family reached out to the Banachi's to help take care of you."

A chill ran up my spine as I remembered all the things I had heard about the Banachi's. They were a rather large family that lived in Chicago but sent their children to a private school in California. They had dealings spread out throughout the US, and their reputation proceeded them. "Mark's family owned a PR firm. How are they connected to the Banachi's?" I asked.

"From what Edge dug up, it appears Mark's grandfather ran into some problems playing the slots quite a few years back, and the Banachi's helped him out. That forged a connection between the families that had only strengthened over time."

"Well, is there any way to get in touch with the Banachi's and explain to them that Marley doesn't want any of this?" Ethel asked as she pushed the foot rest down and sat on the edge of her chair.

"King and Edge are trying to pull some strings and see what they can do. King just called church so that's why you need to pack up and head to the clubhouse with me. I'll feel better if you are somewhere safe," Gravel explained.

I didn't want to go to the clubhouse. I would just end up locked up in Gravel's room, bored out of my mind. "Can't I stay here or go somewhere else that is safe? I could go stay with Gwen. They would never think to look for me there."

"I'm ninety percent sure they know where you work and who you work for, Marley. We don't want to involve any more people in this than we have to. You're coming with me."

"No," I replied, digging my feet in, ready for the fight Gravel was going to give me. "I'll go stay with Troy. I doubt they know about him, it's a perfect idea."

"Marley, no. Just fucking, no," Gravel growled.

"This isn't up for debate, Gravel. Before you walked out of here to answer the phone, I was going to tell you the same thing. You want me to stay with someone, it's Troy or I leave, right now." I stood up and crossed my arms over my chest.

"I need to get to church. I don't have time for this bullshit. The answer is no."

"No need to go to church and figure things out, Gravel. I'll be out of Rockton within the hour." I stepped around Gravel and made my way to the stairs.

"Son of a bitch, Ethel can you talk some fucking sense into her," Gravel hollered as I walked up the stairs.

"I don't see what the problem is with her going to Troy's," I heard Ethel say as I reached the top the stairs and made my way to my room.

"Because it's fucking Cowboy!" Gravel shouted.

Ethel replied, but she talked much quieter than Gravel, and I couldn't make out what she was saying. I reached under my bed and pulled out my suitcase and tossed it on the bed. I rummaged through my drawers, grabbing what I would need and threw it into the suitcase.

I had just opened the closet when Gravel bellowed up the stairs. "You can stay with that fucking cowboy, but you better believe I don't fucking like it!"

A grin spread across my face. I knew all along that as soon as Ethel talked to Gravel about me staying with Troy, he would give in.

I reached into the back of my closet and pulled out the little black dress Troy had bought. When I had tried it on, I didn't plan on buying it, but as soon as Troy had touched me in it, I knew I had to have it. I slipped it off the hanger and folded it, placing it in my suitcase.

Troy's gaze when he had seen me in it had been enough to melt my panties off, well if I had been wearing panties. I grabbed the blood-red heels I had on the floor of my closet and tossed them on top.

It was going to take a lot of talking and begging for Troy to let me in the door. But as soon as he did, I planned on putting my little black dress and heels to good use.

Troy wasn't going to know what hit him.

--*-*-*-*-*-*-*-*-*

Chapter 11

TROY

"Bandit, hurry the hell up," I called as I crossed my arms over my chest, trying to stay warm. It was the beginning of October and Wisconsin had definitely cooled down. Two weeks ago I was walking around in a t-shirt and jeans, and now I almost need to put a god damn parka on.

Bandit bound up the two steps into the house and hopped up on the couch as I shut the door. "I don't know how you can stay out there for so long without your balls freezing off," I mumbled as I cupped my hands together and blew on them. Son of a bitch it was cold out.

It was Friday night, and I thankfully didn't have to work tonight. It was god damn hell at work all week, wanting to ask Meg how Marley was doing but not asking. I was surprised that Meg hadn't mentioned anything more about her either. I had been expecting a full on attack from her about Marley, but she was unusually quiet.

I walked into the kitchen, grabbed two beers and headed back into the living room to catch up on *The Walking Dead*. I had let all of last season's episodes accumulate on my DVR and was slowly watching them on my weekends off.

I sat down on the couch, propping my legs up on the coffee table.

Just as the opening credits started playing, when Meg's ringtone, 'Oath' started blaring from my phone. Meg had snagged my phone and took it upon herself to pick her ringtone for when she called me. She often stole my phone and set random alarms to go off. She thought she was hilarious.

"Meg," I drawled into the phone.

"Don't sound so chipper."

"I'm trying to watch *The Walking Dead*, what do you want?"

"Oh no, I'm interrupting your mutant zombie time," she cackled.

"I'm hanging up in five seconds if you don't tell me why you're calling," I threatened.

"Oh, Troy. Take the stick out of your ass and chill."

"Bye, Meg."

"Wait," she yelled, "I have to tell you something."

I paused the TV and waited for whatever Meg had to tell me. "That is why most people use the telephone, to tell people something."

"You are so fucking cranky lately."

"Meg."

"Fine. You're about to have company in about five minutes. Don't say I didn't warn you."

"What the hell-" I started, but all I heard was silence.

What the hell did she mean I was about to have company. I hoped to hell that wasn't her funny way of telling me that she and Cyn were coming over. I really wasn't up for those two tonight. They maybe my good friends, but sometimes I just want peace and quiet. Their last fiasco of breaking an expensive ass bed still made me laugh and shake my head. Those two were a force of nature when together.

A loud knock sounded on my door, but I didn't get up from the couch. I didn't want anyone to come over. I just wanted to sit on my couch, order some pizza and do nothing. All night. Nothing more, nothing less.

My door rattled as another loud knock landed on the door. Whoever was out there wasn't going away. Bandit's ears perked up, and he turned his head sideways as another loud knock thudded.

"It's probably Meg, boy." He jumped off the couch and raced to the door. Bandit loved Meg. He loved her, even more, when she brought Blue over with her.

Rising from the couch, I walked over to the door and held my hand out to Bandit, and he sat down, waiting for me to open the door.

Just as I was twisting the handle open, the person on the other side pushed on the door, smashing it into my face. Son of a bitch that hurt. I let go of the handle and grabbed my nose, hoping it wasn't bleeding. I tilted my head back and closed my eyes. Why the hell did getting hit in the nose hurt so fucking bad?

"Who the hell stands in front of a door when it's opening?"

Gravel. What in the hell was Gravel doing here? "You pushed the fucking thing into me." I gently prodded my nose, trying to see if it was broken.

"I barely touched you."

"You were thirty seconds in front of us, how did you manage to get a punch in?"

Marley too? What the hell was going on?

"I didn't punch him. Cowboy here was standing in front of the door when he opened it." Gravel walked past me and started walking around the living room.

"You pushed the fucking thing into me."

"Yeah, yeah," Gravel mumbled as he grabbed hold of the banister going upstairs and shook it. He muttered something under his breath as he walked up the stairs.

"I brought your other bag, hun. Are you sure this is enough? Gravel doesn't want you going back to the house until everything is cleared up." I glanced behind Marley and saw Ethel standing behind her.

"I should be okay. I can always do laundry or shop. I've wanted to get some new clothes." Marley walked past me and set the suitcase she was carrying down next to the couch with Ethel following behind her.

I was in the twilight zone. That had to be what was happening.

"There's this little vintage shop that just opened downtown that you should check out. It looks like clothes you would like." Ethel dropped the bag she was carrying and hitched her purse up on her shoulder.

What the fuck was going on? I thought I would never see Marley again, and now here she was, standing in my living room talking to Ethel about vintage clothes.

"We'll have to go there-"

"Stop!" I yelled. I need to know what was going on. To top off all this confusion, my God damn nose was killing me, and I felt a headache coming on.

Ethel and Marley stopped talking and looked at me like I had two heads.

"What the hell are you doing here?"

"Meg said she was going to call and tell you we were on the way over," Ethel said, puzzled why I didn't know what was going on.

"She called me like two fucking minutes ago and told me I was going to have some company. That's it!"

"Oh, no," Marley whispered.

"OK, well, I'll give you the short and sweet condensed story, hun. Marley can fill you in on all the small details later." Ethel plopped down on the couch, and Bandit hopped up next to her, nudging her hand with his nose.

"That would be a good place to start." I slammed the front door shut and crossed my arms over my chest and waited.

"You need to put better locks on all of your windows upstairs and fix this fucking banister." Gravel walked down the stairs, wiggling the banister the whole way. It was more like trying to rip the banister off.

I repeat, what the fuck was going on? Why the hell was Gravel telling me fucking home improvements I needed to do? "The next person who talks better be explaining to me what the hell you are all doing here."

Marley bit her lip and looked at Ethel while she twisted her hands together.

"You ready to go, woman?" Gravel asked as he stood at the bottom of the stairs, his arms folded across his chest.

"Not quite. Meg didn't give Troy the rundown of why Marley is staying, so I think you might want to clue him in on what's going on."

"The assholes who shot at ya'll are mafia. Until we figure shit out, we need someone with her twenty-four seven. Since I missed Marley's rebellion years, she's decided to give me a glimpse of them and insist that she stay with you just to piss me off." Gravel gaze shifted from me to Ethel. "Let's go."

The fucking mafia? Who the hell was Marley engaged to? "For how long? I do have a job."

"Till we get this shit squared away. King said when you're at work, one of the prospects will stay here. Keep her safe or I will fucking kill you." Gravel walked out the door, leaving it open and leaving me still confused as fuck.

"Well, you kids have fun. I'll stop by in a couple of days to see how you two are getting along." Ethel grabbed her purse and followed Gravel out the door. She, at least, shut it behind her.

Marley and I just stared at each other. How the hell did this happen?

--*-*-*-*-*-*-*-*-*

Marley

Troy just stared at me. Not talking, just staring. He didn't look happy to see me. This had all played out so differently in my head. A tense stare down was not what I expected.

"So, I decided to not leave," I said meekly. Start with something positive.

"Why? I thought there was nothing here for you?"

"Ethel and I had a talk, and she helped me to see things clearer. I was making a decision without really thinking things through. I've finally found a place to live that I love, and I've met some amazing people I really don't want to leave behind if I don't have to."

"Why are you here, Marley? There are lots of places you could have stayed that would be as safe as here, if not safer. Four days ago I was someone you could walk away from without a second glance, and now you're at my doorstep expecting me to protect you. I'm sure everything Ethel told you was the same thing I said to you. "

I sat down on the couch, and Bandit hopped up next to me. Bandit seemed to be a bit more forgiving of me than Troy. I scratched behind his ears, and he closed his eyes, leaning into my hand. "I shouldn't have said what I did, Troy. You were right when you said I was irrational, but all that kept playing through my head was that you could have been shot or even worse, killed, because of me. My problems have nothing to do with anyone here, but you all seem to think that you need to fight them for me. I've never had something like that before. Even when I was with Mark, if I had a problem, I solved it, no one else."

"You've had the wrong fucking people in your life, Marley, if they never helped you when you were in trouble." He ran his fingers through his hair and walked over to the TV, pausing the show he was watching.

"You're telling me. I thought Mark's family were upstanding people who did no wrong, and I just found out they have ties to the mafia. That's enough to make me wonder if I've had my head up my ass this whole time and not know who Mark really was either." I turned my head away and dashed away the tears that were streaming down my face.

"None of this is your fault, Marley. I'm sure if there was any indication that Mark was anything less than good, you would have seen it. Don't beat yourself up for something that is out of your control. You had no idea any of this was going to happen when you left California."

"I knew they were upset, but I thought leaving would help. They took me to court to appeal the will ruling, and I'm not fighting it at all. The only reason I can think of as to why they are doing this is because maybe the case isn't going the way they want it to."

Troy sat down on the edge of the recliner and looked at me. "I think it's time we have the conversation about what all happened before you moved to Wisconsin. I can piece together what happened from bits and pieces I've heard, but I'd much rather hear it from you."

"It might take a while," I hiccupped.

Troy popped open the footrest on the chair and reclined back. "I've got all night, Marley. If I'm going to be the one protecting you, I think it's fair I know what I'm protecting you from. Start from the beginning."

I wiped the tears from my eyes and buried my face into Bandit's neck. Telling Troy what was going on was going to be hard, but he had a right to know. A psycho family and the mafia trying to kill me was some serious shit.

"OK," I whispered, sitting back.

Troy held his breath and waited.

--*-*-*-*-*-*-*-*

Chapter 12

Marley

I clenched my hands together and tried to gather my thoughts. Where the hell should I even begin? Bandit laid down, resting his head in my lap. "Mark and I met when I moved to California. We were always in the same classes together but never actually talked until we started high school. Halfway through sophomore year, something changed. He started hanging out by my locker, asking for a pen even though I knew he had one. He finally asked me out on a date right before the end of the school year, and we were inseparable from then on."

"Sounds like your typical high school romance. No red flags ever popped up, made you think there was something up with his family?"

"I knew he had money. His family owns a talent agency and were well known around town. His money never really crossed my mind, because it was his and not mine. His parents hated me the second they met me. They had an air about them that they thought they were better than everyone. We only went over there a couple of times, before his mother called him into the kitchen, and I could hear them arguing about me. I tried to break up with him that night, but he insisted that those were his mother's problems, not his. She had heard about my mom through town gossip. She also knew about Gravel, but I could never figure out how she found out about him. I never talked to anyone about him. I eventually told Mark about Gravel, but he didn't seem to care. Mark was so different from his parents. He didn't really care about money either. Although that could be attributed to the fact that he was so loaded, it was something he was used to." I took a breath and glanced at Troy. His eyes were trained on me, unwavering.

"Keep going, Sunshine," he mumbled when I didn't continue.

I turned away, focusing on the TV in front of me that was paused on three zombies chasing after a woman. Apparently, Troy was also a fan of The Walking Dead. It was also one of my favorite shows, too. "He always wanted to buy me things, but I never wanted them. Half of the jewelry I never wore and put in my dresser. I think one of the things he really liked about me, was that I didn't care about the money. He knew that if the money were gone, I would have still been there. I saw him for who he is, not for what he could buy or give me."

"There's not a lot of women out there like that, Sunshine. I'm glad he saw that you were something special." I was surprised that Troy was being so understanding. Gravel had said if Mark wasn't dead, he would kill him for putting me through this.

"We rarely went to his parents' house, spending most of our time either at my home or just driving around. We were basically inseparable in high school. After we had graduated, he went off to Stanford, and I stayed local, going to community college and recieving my beautician's license."

"You stayed together all the while he was gone?" I knew it was a long time for a couple so young to stay together. Most marriages barely last that long anymore.

"Yeah. He came home to visit once a month. We grew apart somewhat with barely seeing each other, but he was determined to stay with me."

"I bet his folks weren't too happy about that."

"That's the understatement of the year. I very rarely went to his house anymore. After he had graduated college, he came home and started running the family business. We eventually got our own place together, and then he asked me to marry him three years later. I was right in the middle of paying and putting deposits down on rentals and things when he died." Tears were streaming down my face, but I didn't stop talking.

"I got the phone call at seven o'clock at night. He had called before he left the office and told me that he was going to stop at the store to pick up milk and then he would be home. He got hit by a dump truck before he even made it to the shop." I wrapped my arms around my middle and leaned into Bandit. He lifted his head and snuggled into me.

"How long has it been since he passed away?"

"Eight months," I hiccupped. It had been awhile, but not by much.

"I'm sorry."

"I'm normally OK with it, it's just when I have to talk about it, and I seem to lose it." I wiped my nose with the back of my hand and closed my eyes, willing the tears to stop crying.

He kicked the footrest down on his chair and walked into the kitchen and grabbed the box of Kleenex he had on the counter. "Dry your tears, Sunshine."

I grabbed two Kleenex and blew my nose. "His family didn't talk to me until six months after his death when they couldn't get access to his inheritance. I figure they thought that they would be able to get around the clause of all of his belongings and inheritance going to me and ran out of time. As of right now, I own the townhouse Mark and I used to live in and three other properties that were his and a pile of money."

"Holy shit." Troy whistled.

"Yeah, holy shit is right. Although I don't want any of it. I only wanted it if Mark was a part of it. I didn't care about money before he died, and I still don't care about it. I wish his family would just leave me alone."

"So just give it to them and be done with it."

I threw my head back and laughed. "If it were that easy, Troy, I would have done that right away. Mark put a clause that I couldn't give the money away or anything. It's mine, whether I want it or not."

"Fuck."

I wiped my hands on my pants and tried to get my crying under control. "So, that brings us to now."

"Wait, where the hell does the mafia fit in? Did his family hire them?"

"I'm really not sure if they hired them or if it's more of favor. Gravel just told me that Mark's grandfather had gone to the Banachi's for help, and it somehow forged a relationship that hasn't wavered." I leaned forward and grabbed the remote off the coffee table. I was done talking. Troy now knew everything I did, and when I sat back and thought about it, it wasn't a lot.

I hit play on the DVR and sat back, watching an episode of *The Walking Dead* I had already seen. "You're behind almost a full season, Troy."

I glanced at Troy, to see him staring at me. "I don't watch them until I have the full season. I'm a bit behind on watching them, seeing as the new season starts in a week or two."

"Oh, well. I guess I can watch it again with you and try not to tell you what happens." I laughed.

"I hope you're telling me everything, Marley. You know I'm going to talk to King, and if he tells me something you should have, I'm not going to be happy. Now is not the time to be keeping secrets when you're life is on the line," Troy said sternly, his eyes never leaving mine.

"I promise that's it. If King tells you something that I didn't, it's because I didn't know. I had no idea about the whole mafia thing until Gravel told me, I promise." I lifted my hand up and put my other over my heart. 'Scouts Honor."

Troy's eyes traveled over me, scrutinizing me. "You're not leaving?"

I had a lot of mistakes to fix with Troy. I actually had treated him like shit that night I had gotten shot. "I promise I'm not leaving, at least not willingly."

"We'll see." Troy grabbed the remote out of my hand and motioned for me to move over. "Scoot your ass over. The couch is the best place to see the TV from, and even though you've already seen this season of *The Walking Dead,* we're still watching it. The first spoiler that pops out of your mouth, I'm duct taping it and sticking you in the garage."

"You wouldn't dare!" I shrieked, outraged.

"I would, and I have. Just ask Meg. Now scoot your ass over."

"You're an ass if you've ducted taped Meg's mouth shut. Although I'm sure, the thought has also crossed King's mind. She sure is a talker." I slid down to the other side of the couch and leaned against the armrest.

"If he hasn't thought about it, he's a fucking saint. I love Meg to death, but some nights I can't wait to get home and just have silence." Troy pulled the coffee table closer to the couch and kicked his feet up after he sat down.

"She's kind of cool, though," I said, not wanting to sound like I didn't like Meg. I had only known her a short time, but I really liked her.

"Yeah, she's ok," Troy mumbled, turning the TV up.

"Are you trying to silence me subtly by turning the volume up on the TV?" I giggled.

"No, I would never do that," he smirked as he turned it up even louder.

"I'm sorry I'm here interrupting you." I didn't want Troy to hate me for being here. I know he was probably used to being alone at home, and now he had me thrown into his lap.

"You're not. I don't mind you being here, Marley. Now, can we shut up and watch the show?" He glanced over at me, a shit-eating grin on his face.

"You're an ass," I shouted, grabbing the pillow from behind my back and threw it at him.

"I've been told that before. You'll get used to it." He turned his attention back to the TV and relaxed into the couch.

I leaned back into the couch and also turned back to the TV. I didn't want Troy to regret having me here. If he wanted to watch TV and not be disturbed, I'd give him that.

He was, after all, here to protect me. It was the least I could do.

--*-*-*-*-*-*-*

Chapter 13

TROY

"I'm starving," Marley whined from the couch.

I glanced over, seeing her holding her stomach and giving me puppy dog eyes. Did she think that I wasn't going to feed her? I hit the display button on the remote and saw it was past eight o' clock. We had just binged watched six episodes of *The Walking Dead* nonstop, and I was feeling a bit hungry too. "Pizza?"

"Oh my God, hell yes!" Marley screeched, sitting up and bounced on her knees like a kid excited for Christmas morning.

"Bring it down a notch there, Sunshine." I pulled my phone out of my pocket, laughing at Marley. "What do you want on it?"

"Everything. I mean *everything*." She got up and stood in front of my chair, holding her hand out.

"Gross. And what the hell are you holding your hand out for?"

"Give me the phone. Mike knows exactly what I want." She wiggled her fingers at me, waiting for me to hand the phone over.

"Mike, from Pizza Heaven?" I asked. She had only been here for a month. How the hell did she know the owner of Pizza Heaven?

"Yes. I order pizza, at least, three times a week. We've developed quite a relationship. I feel it might be becoming serious."

"He's fucking sixty years old!" I had known Mike for my whole life. I can remember going and eating pizza when I was six. He had a beer gut then, and it still was there. Marley must really love pizza.

"I know, ass. Now, give me the phone." She lunged at me, trying to grab the phone.

I quickly raised my hand over my head and blocked her with my other arm. "You don't know what you're asking for, Sunshine," I warned.

"Yes, I do. I want your phone. It'll be easier if I order." She punched me in the stomach and dove onto the chair with me, trying to reach the phone.

She knocked the wind out of me, but I didn't lower my hand from above my head. Son of a bitch, she played dirty. "You don't play fair," I grunted.

"That's the one thing Gravel taught me that I've never forgotten. Win at all costs." She was sprawled out on top of me, her body flush with mine.

"Even if that means to play dirty," I asked, grabbing her right arm and pinned it behind her back.

"Yes. Even below the belt." She was face to face with me, her lips inches away from mine.

"You're not getting the phone," I vowed.

"Oh yeah? Is that a challenge?"

"No, it's a promise."

"No," she whispered. I leaned forward, closing the gap between us, and brushed my lips against her's.

"I've missed you," she moaned.

"Me too, Sunshine." I deepened the kiss, savoring the feel and taste of her. Son of a bitch did I miss Marley. I tried telling myself for the past few days that she was just a one night stand, but there was no denying the chemistry and pull we had for one another. I released her arm from behind her back and grabbed her ass. I forgot how good she felt in my arms.

"Mmm, you play dirty, too, Troy," she whispered in between kisses.

"I told you not to mess with me."

"If this is me messing with you, I think I'll do this regularly." She delved her fingers into my hair and pressed her lips against mine. I opened my mouth, wanting to taste all of her. She slipped her tongue into my mouth, and I moaned, loving what she was giving to me.

"You forgot one thing," she whispered, pulling away.

"What's that?" I asked, my hand traveling up her back and gripped the back of her neck. I pulled her towards me, needing more.

"You forgot I play below the belt." That was all I had heard before I saw stars flash before my eyes and Marley grabbed my semi-erect dick and twisted.

"Son of a bitch," I yelped, bucking my hips trying to get out of her hold. Marley reached up with her other hand and ripped the phone out of my hand I forgot I was holding.

She pushed off of me and stood up. Marley just grabbed my family jewels and grabbed them like her life depended on it. I reached down, rubbing my crotch and growled at her. "That was dirty."

"You should have just given me the phone," she sang out as she swiped left and started pressing buttons.

"I'm not going to forget about that anytime soon. Payback is a bitch, Sunshine." I kicked the footrest closed on the chair and leaned forward in the chair, my hand not leaving my dick just in case Marley came back for more.

"I have no doubt about that, but you have to catch me first." She winked at me and walked into the kitchen, the phone held to her ear.

I rubbed my dick, the throbbing pain diminishing. How the hell did I not see that coming? Usually, I could read people and know what they were going to do, but not with Marley. The second her lips had touched mine, all common sense had fled, and all I could think about was how she felt.

I shook my head and stood up. This just went to show I needed to have my guard up when it came to Marley. She could fuck me up, and I wouldn't even see it coming.

I heard her laugh ring out and the words, 'everything, even the anchovies.' I had better get that phone out of her hand, or I wouldn't be eating anything tonight if she put fucking anchovies on the pizza. "No anchovies, Sunshine," I called as I turned the TV off and headed to the kitchen. "I don't want all that garbage on my pizza."

"You'll eat whatever I order." She stuck her tongue out at me and dashed around to the other side of the table.

She mumbled into the phone and then tossed it to me. "I can always call and cancel whatever the hell you just ordered."

"You wouldn't dare." She cocked her hip out and rested her hand on it. God dammit Marley looked good. After that kiss she gave me, my fucking brain was fried. All I could think about was how to get close to her again.

"I can and would. What's stopping me from doing it? How bad do you want your pizza?"

Her eyes bugged out, and she swallowed hard. "You're holding my pizza hostage?"

"If I don't get something in return, yes." I swiped the screen, unlocking it and pulled up the number to Pizza Heaven.

"Wait!" Marley yelled. My finger hovered over the send button. "Name your price."

A grin spread across my face. Looked like tonight was about to get a whole lot more interesting.

--*-*-*-*-*-*-*

Chapter 14

Marley

Troy just stood there smirking at me. Smug bastard. I was starving and would do basically anything for my favorite food. Maybe if I distracted him long enough, the pizza would get here before he named his price and then I wouldn't have to do it.

"You ok with getting wet?"

Heat spread across my cheeks, and I knew my face was bright red. Holy shit, right to the point. "Uh, I guess so."

"The whole time you're here, I want you..." He trailed off.

I waited, knowing what he was about to say but needed to hear it. "Do what?" I whimpered.

He grabbed my hand, turning it over in his, swirling patterns with his finger tip. "I typically don't ask girls to do this for me," he whispered, leaning into me. His mouth inches away from my ear.

A shiver ran through my body, a whimper escaped my lips. "Tell me," I pleaded.

"The whole time you're here..."

"Yes." I gripped his biceps, dying to hear the words come out of his mouth. I wanted Troy, but I needed to hear that he wanted me too.

"I want you to do the dishes."

"Me too, I've-." Wait, what the hell did he just say?

"Thanks, Sunshine." He grinned, stepping back. "You might want to start the water and get some of those soaking before the pizza comes. We're out of plates, and those have been sitting there for a couple of days." He tapped me on the ass and sprinted up the stairs.

What the bloody fuck? Dishes? I made a fool of myself getting all hot and bothered and then he tells me he needs me to do the dishes. Son of a bitch. What an ass.

This was war.

--*-*-*-*-*-*-*-*-*

TROY

I was two seconds away from telling Marley what I really wanted her to do but changed my mind at the last second. Marley may have said she was planning on staying, but she had said that before. I wanted Marley in my bed more than anything, but I wasn't about to fall for her and then have her leave.

She looked ready to kill when I smacked her ass and ran up the stairs. If looks could kill, I'm pretty sure I never would have made it up the stairs.

I flipped on the light to my room and walked over to the bed and sat down. I listened, hearing pots and pans being slammed on the counter and water running.

I had to give her credit. She was actually attempting to do the dishes. Right before I was ready to tell her just how wet I was about to get her, I had glimpsed the stack of dirty dishes behind her and chickened out. At least this way the dishes would be clean. The banging and clanging from downstairs grew louder, and a grin spread across my lips.

The dishes may be clean, but I was going to have one pissed off Marley on my hands.

--*-*-*-*-*-*-*-*-*

Chapter 15

Marley

I knew he wanted me. I could tell he was just as affected as I was when we were close. Why he kept denying it and backing away was beyond me.

I watched him from my end of the couch as he ate. I was sitting sideways, my plate in my lap, my eyes glued to him. After he had come downstairs doing God knows what, I had somewhat cooled off and came up with a battle plan.

He was running. I could see it. I wasn't going to let him run anymore. Every time he would try to step back, I was going to be right there behind him.

"You want the last slice?" I blinked, realizing I had totally spaced out and shook my head no.

Just as the pizza had gotten here, I had finished up the dishes and was wiping down the counters when Troy had opened the door. I stood up, grabbed the empty box and headed into the kitchen.

"Marley," Troy called.

"Yeah."

"You don't need to clean up anymore, Sunshine."

I rolled my eyes thinking he was the ass who had told me in the first place I had to wash the dishes. Plus, I didn't expect to stay here without doing my share of cleaning. "I know." I opened the freezer, spotting the box of Twix ice cream bars I had seen when I was snooping around, waiting for the sink to fill.

"Catch." I tossed Troy one and plopped down on the couch.

We had just finished the last episode of *The Walking Dead* and now he was scrolling through, trying to find a movie to watch on Netflix.

"*Speed*?"

"No." Keanu was hot, but not in the mood.

"*The Expendable's*?"

"No." Didn't even know what the hell that was.

"You're making this impossible. You've shot down the last five movies I've said." Troy bitched.

"That's because you're not saying any I want to watch. Give me the remote." I demanded.

He turned his head to me and smirked. "Fat chance of that happening."

"Remember what happened about an hour ago to your junk?" I asked, making a fist with my hand.

Troy cringed, tossed me the remote and put a hand on his dick. "I don't think my balls can take any more abuse tonight."

"Wise choice," I murmured flipping through the movies.

"You put a chick flick on, guarantee I will be passed out in ten minutes."

"How about we compromise. *50 First Dates*? I get my chick flick, but it's got Adam Sandler in it, so it's, at least, funny."

"Fine, but next time I get to pick the movie, and it's going to be whatever the hell I want it to be."

"Deal." I grabbed the pillow from the end of the couch and threw it at Troy.

"What the hell are you doing?"

"Getting comfy," I said as I laid my head down on the pillow in Troy's lap.

"What if I wanted to lie down?" He looked down at me, a scowl on his face.

"Then lay down." I leaned forward, letting him get up but his arm clamped around my middle and pulled my back down.

"I don't want to." He left his arm wrapped around me and kicked his feet up on the coffee table.

"You're an ass. What the hell did you ask for?" I grabbed the blanket off the back of the couch and draped it over me.

"Cause I'm an ass. Watch the movie," he said, shushing me.

I turned over my side facing the TV and tried to focus on the movie, not Troy's arm wrapped around me or how close he was.

Halfway through the movie, I felt my eyes start to get heavy and cuddled up even more to Troy. I had planned on getting all touchy with him, trying to knock down his defenses, but it seemed like too much work right now.

Tomorrow I definitely was going to put my plan into motion. Tonight, sleep seemed all I was capable of. Five minutes later I was out.

--*-*-*-*-*-*-*

Chapter 16

TROY

It was seven o'clock, and I was awake. What the hell? I never woke up before ten on Saturday. Hell, most days I wasn't up before ten.

I had been staring at the clock on the wall for the past ten minutes, listening to Marley's slow breathing. I had to pee like a god damn race horse but didn't want to wake up Marley.

Half way through the movie she had fallen asleep and I wasn't very far behind her by the time I passed out. Sleeping with my head tilted all the way back and cocked to the right gave me a pounding headache and a stiff neck.

I needed coffee and Tylenol, stat.

Marley's eyes fluttered, and she stretched out in my arms. "What time is it?" she mumbled, turning over to look up at me.

"Just after seven."

"Ugh, I have to get ready for work. There's a bridal party coming in at eight that I need to help with. Gwen will kill me if I'm not there." Marley sat up, running her fingers through her hair and stretched her arms over her head. The back of her shirt rode up, exposing her smooth back. My fingers itched to touch her, but she was up and in the kitchen before I could do something stupid like grab her and never let go.

I scrubbed my hands down my face and stood up. Time to get the day started and try to keep my hands off Marley.

--*-*-*-*-*-*

Marley

I looked out the shop window and saw Troy sitting in his truck, his sunglass covered eyes trained on the salon. After Troy had shown me my room, I had gotten dressed and ready in record time.

As I was walking out the door to my car, Troy scared the shit out of me when he grabbed my elbow and guided me over to his truck. He told me he would be driving me to and from work from now on.

After a five minute argument that basically boiled down to me calling Troy an ass fifty times and my butt planted in his truck while he drove me to work. Apparently, Gravel had called while I was getting ready and told Troy that everyone was busy at the club today, and he would need to be my personal bodyguard for the day.

Not exactly how I wanted Troy to be with me. I didn't want him to start resenting me because I kept getting tossed into his lap.

"Is he going to sit there all morning?" Gwen asked, peering over my shoulder at Troy.

"More than likely. I should probably take him some coffee or something," I murmured.

"Not a bad idea, although you have Mrs. Jenkins coming in during the bridal party. You might want to get your station set up. I can take him coffee." Gwen grabbed an empty coffee cup, filled it and was out the door before I could say anything.

She pranced across the street and knocked on Troy's window. Man, I wish I could know what Troy was thinking right now. Gwen was in rare form today. She looked like a sexed up fifties housewife.

Her hair was piled on top of her head, and her face was painted flawlessly, and her bright red lips looked amazing. The navy blue dress with white polka dots all over it hugged her curves in all the right places and made me wish I had the balls to dress like her. Gwen was a definite rockabilly with attitude to match.

I couldn't see what Troy's face looked like when he saw Gwen, but I'm sure he was impressed by her. Hell, I liked guys, and I was impressed by her.

"Am I early?"

I turned around, seeing Mrs. Jenkins walking in through the back door. Mrs. Jenkins was Gwen's upstairs tenant who owned the salon before Gwen took it over. She had owned the salon for over thirty years before she had to give it up. Gwen's aunt lived in Rockton and was good friends with Mrs. Jenkins. When the salon had gone up for sale, Gwen snatched it up before it even went on the market.

"No, not at all Barb. Have a seat at my station and I'll get you started." I motioned, tearing my eyes away from the window. I was torturing myself watching Gwen and Troy together.

As I was chatting Barb up about everything that had happened the past couple of weeks, Gwen walked back in with the bridal party right behind her.

I glanced out the window, trying to catch a glimpse of Troy, but he wasn't in his truck anymore. "Just one sec," I mumbled to Barb.

I walked to the window and looked up and down the street trying to see Troy.

"Looking for something?"

I whirled around at the sound of Troy's voice right by my ear. How the hell had he gotten in here without me knowing it? "How the hell did you get in here?" I swear to god I almost shit myself.

"I told Gwen I was going to walk around the building and check things out," Troy smirked at me, knowing I should probably go check my pants.

"Did checking the building include scaring the ever living shit out of me?" I stepped back, trying to get away from him and backed right into the window. Ouch.

"Trying to get away from me, Marley?" He stepped forward, caging me in with his arms.

"No, I just have work to do." Danger Will Robinson, DANGER!

"How come you sent Gwen out with coffee?"

Huh? I didn't do anything. Gwen couldn't get out the door fast enough. "I didn't send Gwen, she's just nice," I mumbled. Gwen was nice, but her motive for wanting to take Troy coffee was anything but nice. More like to check out Troy.

"Hmm, not sure if I believe that."

He just stared at me, not moving. I couldn't tell what he was thinking or what he wanted me to do. I was utterly clueless about everything. "I really need to get back to work, Troy. I need to finish up Barb and then help Gwen. I should be done by noon if you want to just wait for me out in your truck." Yes, please go to your truck. Troy was a distraction I didn't need while I was at work.

"I think I'll just wait over there, can never be too careful." Troy pointed to the small waiting area Gwen had at the front of the shop. Thankfully, from my station, I couldn't see the waiting area, so that would work. As long as I couldn't see Troy, I would be able to work. Maybe.

"OK. You sit over there, and I'm going to stay here. Or well, over there," I muttered, pointing to my station.

"OK, Sunshine. After work, I have a surprise. You got clothes at my house that can get dirty, possibly ruined?"

What an odd question. I thought about what was in my suitcase. I guess I could scrounge up something that could work. "Sure. What are we doing?"

"It's a surprise. Now, hurry up and make these women pretty so we can get the hell out of here." Troy's hand came up and tipped my head back. His lips hovered inches away from mine.

"I'm at work," I whispered. I wanted to kiss Troy more than anything, but work PDA was not something I was into.

"I know." He closed the gap between us, brushing his lips against mine in a quick kiss. "Hurry up."

He turned away, walking to the waiting area and grabbed a magazine off the table and started flipping through it.

I looked around, seeing everyone's eyes were on me. Shit. There goes my rule of no work PDA. I cleared my throat and walked back over to Barb, trying to act like I wasn't affected by Troy at all.

"Hold onto that one tight and don't let him go, sweetheart," Gwen quietly said as I walked by her station.

"Amen, sister." Barb agreed.

Everyone burst out laughing, and my cheeks heated and turned bright red. I glanced over at Troy to see if he had heard. A smirk was playing his lips as he paged through a magazine. A magazine, might I add, that was upside down.

Maybe Troy wasn't as unaffected as I had thought.

--*-*-*-*-*-*-*-*-*

Chapter 17

TROY

"So are you going to tell me what we are doing?" Marley asked from the passenger seat.

After she had gotten off work, we headed back to my house where we both changed into crappy clothes that could get dirty and hopped back in the truck with Bandit sitting in between us.

"You'll see once we get there."

"I'm sure I will, but it would be nice to know what it is we are doing before we get there."

I shook my head and didn't say anything. I had no idea if Marley was going to like my surprise. I guess it was kind of a test to see if she was a chick I could see myself being with.

"Can you, at least, tell me if I'm dressed OK?" she demanded.

I looked at her ripped jeans and black Henley and knew she was dressed perfectly for what I had in mind. "You'll do."

"Ugh!" Marley sighed, crossing her arms over her chest and turned to pout out the window.

This could get interesting.

--*-*-*-*-*-*

Marley

"Where are we?" I asked as we drove down a dirt road.

"Just keep watching."

This was ridiculous. Why the hell couldn't he tell me where we were going? I had gone along with his little game this long, I guess five more minutes wasn't going to kill me, although it sure felt like it would.

The gravel road was surrounded by trees and brush. It was fall, and all the leaves on the trees had turned red, orange, and yellow, and it was beautiful. We crossed over a wooden bridge and then came to a clearing where a huge garage stood.

"I still have no idea what we are doing."

"One more minute, Marley, and you'll know. You really don't handle surprises very well." He laughed, shaking his head.

That was an understatement. I hated surprises unless I was the one giving the surprise. I hated being out of the loop, not knowing what was going on. "Fifty seconds," I called as he got out of the truck.

He walked over to my side of the truck and opened my door. "How open minded are you?"

"Very. To a point."

"What the breaking point of not being open to things?"

"Surprise threesomes."

Troy's jaw dropped open, and he was speechless. "How did... has someone...wow, that's..." Troy sputtered.

"Is there a threesome waiting behind that garage door Troy?" I asked, trying not to laugh.

"Hell no!"

"Good, now get out of my way so I can see what the surprise is," I insisted, trying to push him to the side.

"No. Just stand in front of the overhead door. I need to go in and open it from the inside. Promise me you'll wait."

His eyes held mine captive, waiting for me to promise. "Haven't I waited long enough?"

"You have, but it'll be a better surprise if you wait."

"Dammit, fine. You go, open the door, and I'll wait here like a good little girl."

Troy leaned in, "Don't you know good little girls always get rewarded?" His lips touched mine, giving me what I had been craving. I reached up, delving my fingers into his hair and held on.

His lips caressed mine, and I moaned. God dammit could Troy kiss. "This isn't part of my plan, Marley," he whispered against my lips.

"Oh well. Forget your plan." His arms were wrapped around me, and his fingertips were drawing lazy circles on my back. I turned on the seat, putting a leg on each side of Troy and pulled him flush against me.

"Why can't I say no to you? Even when I know I should," he mumbled, pressing kisses along my neck. I tilted my head to the side, giving him better access and hummed under my breath. No matter what Troy's surprise was, it wasn't going to be able to top this.

"Because I can't say no to you either. Maybe we should both stop trying."

"First, your surprise and then no more saying no to me." He placed one last kiss on my neck and stepped back.

"How long is the surprise going to take?" I asked, catching my breath. I repeat, kissing Troy was incredible.

"Depends on how much you like it. Could be ten minutes or hours." He held his hand out and helped me down from the truck and slammed the door shut behind us.

"Now I want to know even more what it is. Go open the damn door," I ordered, pushing him away.

Troy laughed and jogged over to the side of the building and disappeared. I glanced around seeing we were surrounded by beautiful trees with trails cut into them, taking a person Lord knows where. There was a tire swing hanging off one of the trees and a couple of chairs gathered around a fire pit to the left. It was gorgeous and peaceful.

"You ready?" Troy yelled from inside the garage.

"Hell yes! Open the door!" I yelled back.

The door slowly raised revealing Troy standing on the other side. I shielded my eyes from the sun and peered into the garage.

"Your messy garage is my surprise? Don't tell me you brought me here to help organize it. I will walk my happy ass back to town if that's the case," I ranted.

Troy threw his head back and laughed. "No, Sunshine, I did not bring you here to clean the garage. Besides, it's not messy."

"Mhmm, sure." I nodded my head and smirked.

"You're surprise is right here." Troy walked over to a four wheeler and patted the seat.

"We're going four wheeling?" I asked excitedly.

"Do you want to?"

"Hell to the yes!" I shouted, jumping up and down. I freaking loved four wheeling. One of my friends back in California had four wheelers, and we would always take them out and tear up her lawn. It was fucking awesome. I hadn't done it in years.

Troy tossed me a helmet and grabbed one for himself. "Strap that on, Sunshine, and show me what you got."

Oh, I definitely planned on show him what I had. Now and tonight.

--*-*-*-*-*-*-*

Chapter 18

TROY

I was blown away by the fact that Marley liked to four-wheel, let alone knew what one was. She didn't seem like the type of girl who liked to get dirty, but she was proving me wrong by ripping it up on all the trails.

I had taken her to the five acres of property I had bought three years ago. Two years ago I had built the huge garage that had a small apartment in the back. We were only less than half an hour away from town, but it was nice sometimes to get away.

We had been riding the trails for the past hour when I had pulled over by the small river that ran through the property, thinking Marley would stop too. She again proved me wrong by flying past me, her blonde hair floating behind her. "One more time!" I heard her yell.

She roared off down the trail that would loop around back to the river, and I decided to just sit and wait for her.

Five minutes later I heard her roar back down the path, and she slammed on the brakes when she pulled up next to me.

"This is the best day ever!" She yelled as she turned her four wheeler off.

"So, I take it you like your surprise?" I laughed.

"It's ok," she smirked.

"You want to head over to the apartment and get something to drink?" I asked.

"Apartment?"

"Yeah, it's on the other side of the garage. Come on, I'll show you." I cranked back up my four-wheeler and drove back to the apartment with Marley close behind me.

I pulled up to the cement slab patio I had on the other side of the building and killed the engine.

"Wow, you can't even tell this is a garage on this side," Marley said, awed as she pulled up next to me and turned off her four wheeler.

This side of the building I had sided with split logs and there was a large awning that spanned the whole side. "Thanks. I stay here when I need to get away."

"We're barely out of town, but it feels like we're hours away. This is awesome. It's like a staycation that doesn't feel like a staycation." Marley hopped off and walked over to the rocking chair I had by the front door and plopped down on it.

"I'm gonna grab us a drink and then you are going to tell me what the hell a staycation is."

"Wait for me, I wanna see what the inside looks like." Marley jumped up and followed me into the apartment.

I flipped the lights on, illuminating the wide open layout.

"There aren't any walls," Marley marveled as she wandered into the middle of the room.

There really wasn't any walls beside the one separating the apartment from the garage. As you walked through the door, the kitchen was to your right. The counter and cabinets lined half of the wall, and there was an L-shaped island that gave the kitchen some definition of space.

Past the kitchen was the bedroom that had a king size bed with a chest at the foot and a dresser on the wall.

The bathroom was kitty corner from us, taking up the far left corner. This was the only space with walls. When I was building the garage/apartment, I had planned on no walls at all, but Meg had convinced me of at least putting a wall around the toilet. She had wanted me to do the whole bathroom, but I had compromised with just enclosing in the toilet. The floor was tiled with a large claw foot tub with a shower curtain that surrounded the whole thing. The sink was next to the tub and the "toilet stall" was in the corner.

To the right was the living room where I had bought a huge overstuffed L-shaped sectional, and there was a recliner on each side of it. I had a sixty inch TV hanging on the wall and surround sound speakers placed all around the loft. Hey, I was a guy. Yes, the TV was the most impressive thing.

"Wow, you can't even tell we are in a garage." Marley wandered over to the bathroom and peeked into the toilet stall.

"That's because we aren't in a garage. We're in an apartment that is attached to a garage." I walked over to the fridge and grabbed a beer. I had no clue what Marley was going to want to drink. Meg had left some of her girl drinks here, so I grabbed one of those for her too.

"You know what I mean. This is really cool."

"Yeah, it's a roof over my head when I don't feel like going home." I opened the door, and Bandit came running in, skidding to a stop in the bedroom. "Come get a drink boy," I called, bending over to grab his bowl and filled it with water.

"Is that for me?" Marley asked, pointing to the wine cooler in my hand.

"Yeah, that shit is too sweet for me." I popped the top and handed it to her.

"I can't picture you drinking anything but beer," Marley mused, eyeing me up and down.

"Beer and whiskey. That's it."

"Hmm, straight up whiskey?"

"The only way to drink it." I took a pull of my beer and set it down on the island. I leaned back against the counter and crossed my arms over my chest.

"So, what do we do now?"

"Whatever you want. We can head back to my house if you want."

"Or, we could stay here." Marley walked over to me, setting her drink next to mine and stood in front of me.

"We could." Marley's eyes roamed my body up and down while she bit her lip. Son of a bitch. Marley was just looking at me, and I was already pitching half a tent. She reached out, fingering one of the buttons on my shirt and licked her lips.

"Do you want to play a game?" She whispered, stepping closer. I spread my legs, and she stepped in between them.

"What kind of game?" I husked out, not recognizing my own voice.

"The one where we see if all this sexual tension between us will be explosive as I've been imaging." Her voice was husky and laced with lust.

I reached up and tucked the hair that was cascading around her face behind her ear. "Doesn't sound like a game to me. How will we know who the winner is?" Smooth, Troy. Marley was literally throwing herself at me, and I was wondering about the rules of the game.

She leaned up and whispered in my ear, "That's the thing, Troy, we play this right, and we'll both be the winner."

"Game on." I pushed Marley back, put my shoulder in her stomach and lifted her up.

"Ahh! Troy! What the hell!" Marley screeched.

"Shh, it's a short walk," I said, slapping her ass. I strode over to the bed and tossed her onto it.

She flailed on the bed, bouncing up and down. She propped her elbows behind her and pushed her hair out of her face. "I should be pissed you just threw me, but I just can't get over how sexy that was."

"Good, I'd much rather have you sexed up then bitching at me." I toed my cowboy boots off and pushed them under the bed.

Marley slipped her's off to and tossed them over the side of the bed. "Take your shirt off. It was too dark the last time. This time, I want to see what I'm touching."

I tugged my shirt up over my head and tossed it on the floor. "Now your's," I ordered.

She grabbed the bottom hem and slowly tugged it up, exposing her perfect skin inch by inch. Her perfect tits were encased in a blood red bra with black piping. "Red," I growled.

"It is your favorite color if I do remember correctly," she purred cupping her tits, pushing them together, almost presenting them to me.

"Any color you wear is my favorite," I growled. I couldn't take it anymore, I needed to touch her.

I stepped forward, my knees hitting the edge of the bed. I crawled up the bed, caging Marley in underneath me. "You still have your pants on."

"Oh trust me, Sunshine, they won't be on for long." I reached over, my fingertips brushing the strap off. She shivered under my light touch and wrapped her arms around my neck.

"I trust you, Troy," she whispered. I leaned down, dropping my body on top of her's and sealed her lips with mine.

I sat back on my ass, raising Marley with me, our lips still touching. Reaching behind her, I quickly unhooked her bra and tossed it with the rest of our discarded clothes.

"You need to take your pants off. Now," she demanded, scrambling to her knees and grabbed the button on my jeans. She popped the button open and slid the zipper down slowly, I was in pure agony with each click of the zipper as she pulled it down.

"Lay back down," I ordered. Her hands came up, covering herself before I could get a glimpse of her perfect tits. "Put your arms down."

Marley shook her head no and laughed. "Not until you take your pants off." She laid back, her arms crossed over her chest.

"How about I take your pants off instead?" I grabbed each leg of her pants and tugged.

"You need to unbutton them," she giggled as I started pulling her down the bed.

"No, you need to undo them and show me those perfect nipples I remember."

"Nope, not happening until your pants come off."

I leaned forward, easily popping open the button and slid the zipper down. "I'll just have to take matters into my own hands," I growled, grabbing the waist of her jeans and tugged them down.

She had matching panties on that were bright red and tiny black polka dots all over them. I leaned down, my face right in front of her pussy and placed a kiss right where I knew her sweet clit was. She bucked her hips at me wanting more. I looked up, seeing her pretty eyes pointed at me, desire clouding them.

"Let me see those pretty tits, Marley." She shook her head no, a grin stretching across her lips. Little tease.

I leaned back and tugged her jeans down the rest of the way. I stood up, my jeans sliding down but got hung up on my dick. I pushed them down, my dick bobbing and throbbing under the thin material of my boxers.

"Boxers, too," Marley breathed out.

I hooked my thumbs in the waistband and tugged them down, letting them fall to the floor. "Now let me see those tits, Sunshine."

I crawled up the bed, straddling Marley in between my legs and pulled her arms down to her sides. I leaned down, running kisses over the swell of her breasts and heard her shallow breaths.

"Troy," she moaned as I sucked her nipple into my mouth. She arched her chest into me, begging for more.

I let go of her arms, one hand tweaking her nipple and the other reaching for the waistband of her underwear. "You have too many clothes on," I mumbled.

She reached down, scrambling to rip them off. "Slow down, Sunshine," I murmured, leaning back, kneeling in between Marley's spread legs. I stilled her hands and raised them up to my mouth, kissing them. "Let me."

I grabbed the band of her underwear and slowly pulled them down, exposing her sweet pussy. She arched her hips, allowing me to pull them off, and I tossed them on the floor. Leaning down, I rubbed her smooth mound and growled. Son of a bitch, Marley sure was something else. I had never had a woman spread out before me so perfect. "I need you, Troy."

"I'm right here, baby," I parted the lips of her pussy and saw her glistening clit begging for attention. "This is mine."

"Yes," she moaned as I leaned down and flicked her clit with the tip of my tongue. Her hips bucked, asking for more. "Please," Marley pleaded.

"You're my greedy little girl."

"Yes, god yes," she moaned as I sucked her clit into my mouth, savoring her flowery scent and addicting taste. I circled her clit with my tongue feeling her squirm. I trailed a hand up her body, pressing a hand on her stomach, holding her down.

"Calm down, baby. We've got a long way to go," I taunted, nipping her clit. She screamed out, gripping my shoulders, digging her fingernails into my back. I groaned, loving the feel of her nails biting into my back. Marley was a wildcat in bed.

I stroked her clit, hearing her cries of ecstasy as she climbed higher and higher, closer to her release. My finger replaced my tongue, flicking her clit even faster, her legs pushing her body off the bed.

I slid up her body, nipping at her tits, swirling my tongue around her pert nipples. "Troy, I'm so close!" Marley yelled, throwing her head back into the pillow.

"That's right, baby, you're going to cum on my hand and then your tight little pussy is going to cum around my hard dick," I growled into her ear. I wrapped my hand around her neck and pulled her close.

I pinched her clit, and her body exploded around me, bucking wildly, moaning in pleasure. Her eyes rolled back in her head, and she wrapped her arms around me, taking everything I gave her. I gently stroked her clit, slowly bringing her down. "You're so fucking sweet, baby girl," I said, praising her. I rubbed slow circles over her mound as she purred with satisfaction. Fucking perfect, and we were only getting started.

--*-*-*-*-*-*-*-*-*-*-*

Marley

Holy shit. Like, totally holy shit. I had never felt anything like that before in my life. I was laying limp beneath Troy, and I highly doubted I would be able to move for the next hour.

"You're my little wildcat," Troy mumbled, running kisses down my neck.

"Wildcat?"

"Yeah, baby, I'm pretty sure you left your mark on me." I opened my eyes and looked at Troy. What was he talking about?

"I'm not following, Troy. If anyone left their mark, it was you. I'm pretty sure you have broken me, but I don't want to be fixed." I wrapped my arms around his back, trailed my fingers up and down.

"Look at my back, baby girl. Fucking drove me crazy when your nails dug into me." I lifted my head and saw perfect little crescent moon shapes on his shoulders.

Holy hell. I didn't even remember doing that. I lined my nails up with the indents and squeezed.

"Hmm, fuck yeah. Just like that, wildcat," Troy growled, nipping my ear.

"Remember what you said about me coming on your hand?' I asked, rolling my head to the left, giving Troy better access. He nodded his head and continued kissing me. "Well, I'm ready to come around your dick now," I purred feeling my body tightening just from his kisses.

"Fucking perfect," he whispered in my ear. He leaned back, kneeling in between my legs and looked down at me.

I spread my legs wide, digging my heels into the mattress. He grabbed his dick and stroked it as he spread my pussy open with the other hand. He flicked my clit and my body hummed from his touch. I needed Troy now. "Please," I pleaded, not above begging anymore.

He leaned forward, his rock hard dick sliding up and down my slick pussy. "I had you before, Sunshine, but now you're mine."

"Please," I pleaded. Every time his dick stroked my clit, tremors ran through my body, and I felt like I was ready to explode.

He lined up his cock with my drenched pussy and slowly pushed in. I tilted my hips, begging for more. "Faster," I pleaded.

"We'll get there, baby girl. If I go any faster, this is going to be over before it even gets started," he gritted out through clenched teeth. His hands were gripping my legs, fingertips digging into me.

He slid all the way in and closed his eyes. I had never seen a more gorgeous man than in this moment. A drop of sweat trickled down his brow, slid down his neck. His arms and neck were tensed from trying to keep control. I clenched the walls of my pussy, and a pained expression crossed his face. "You do that one more time, Marley, I'm going to bend you over my knee and spank the hell out of you."

"Promise," I purred picturing Troy's handprint on my ass. He slapped my leg, drawing me out of my daydream.

"Stop, you're doing it again," he growled.

I hadn't even noticed I was doing it. I was so turned on, my body was taking over. Troy's rock hard dick inside me was driving me insane. Shit! Troy's rock hard dick with NO CONDOM! "Stop!" I screeched, pushing at his chest. "You forgot the condom."

"Son of a bitch," Troy grumbled, pulling out. "Sorry, Sunshine," he apologized and leaned over the side of the bed and grabbed his pants off the floor. He found his wallet, flipped it open and tossed the condom to me.

"So I need to put this on you?" I hummed, ripping the package open with my teeth and pulled it out. Troy crawled back over to me, his dick bobbing at me. I rolled the condom on his dick, pulsing under my fingertips.

"I think we're good now," I purred, stroking his dick in my hand.

"I think we're more than good," he growled, pushing me back on the bed and spread my legs out. He slowly slid

143

into me again, stroking in and out. "Fuck, you feel good, Marley."

"Faster," I pleaded.

Troy sped up, my walls clenching around him as he drove me to the edge again. He reached down, flicked my clit with his thumb and my hips bucked, a spasm running through me. "More."

"So fucking greedy, baby girl." He flicked my clit harder, almost to the brink of pain. I closed my eyes and tossed my head back as fireworks exploded behind my eyelids. Troy leaned forward, caging me in with his arms, his body pressing me into the bed as he pistoned into me, finding his own release. He threw his head back, letting out a cry of ecstasy and slammed into me one more time.

All I could hear was the pounding of my heart in my ears as I came down from heaven. Troy collapsed on me, his breathing heavy and labored.

"Holy fuck," he sighed, burying his face in the crook of my neck.

"Yes, definitely holy fuck." I agreed, giggling.

"Laughing while my dick is still in you, Sunshine, is not a big ego boost," he mumbled.

"I think your ego is just fine." I stroked his back, gently scratching my nails up and down.

"Hmm, you can do that all night, Sunshine."

"Oh my god! My eyes! My eyes! I'm scared!"

Troy jumped, his arms wrapping around me. "What the fuck?" he yelled.

I peeked over his shoulder and saw Meg standing at the door that was thrown wide open, her hand covering her eyes.

"Oh. My. God. I'm blind! I can't unsee that!" Meg screeched.

"Then get the fuck out!" Troy bellowed!

"Babe, what the hell? Why didn't you knock?" I heard King growl.

"I did! They didn't fucking hear me!"

"Oh my god," I wheezed out, laughing.

"Have you ever heard of locking doors? I did not need to see your lily white ass waving in the air. I think I might be blind. Oh my God, I'm blind, Lo!"

I leaned forward looking over Troy's shoulder just in time to see Meg whip around and walk straight into King, almost knocking them both over.

"Can you both leave until we get our damn clothes on?" Troy yelled, annoyed.

"Yes! I'm getting the fuck out!" Meg yelled back, her head buried in King's chest. King walked out backward, Meg pushing him and she slammed the door shut.

I burst out laughing, my body shaking. "You think this is funny, Sunshine?"

I nodded my head, unable to talk. I had just had the best sex of my life and moments later Meg and King walks through the door. I was beyond embarrassed, but it was funny as hell.

"Do you think Meg will ever see again?" I laughed.

"Fuck she's crazy. Acts like it's my fault she walks in on us and then insults me on top of it, too. I can't help it my ass is white. This is Wisconsin, who the hell tans their ass?" Troy rolled off of me and sprawled out on the other side of the bed.

"It is pretty white," I teased, leaning over and placing a kiss on his chest. "How long do you think they are going to give us before they come back in?"

"I think with King holding her off we have at least fifteen minutes before she comes barging back in." Troy leaned up on his elbows and kissed my forehead. "You have something in mind you want to do in those fifteen minutes, Sunshine?"

I swung my leg over and straddled Troy's hips. "I plan on getting very, very wet," I purred, grinding on him.

"I think I can help with that." Troy threw his arms behind his head and relaxed back, watching me.

"Oh yeah? I guess you can grab the soap for me," I sang out as I scrambled off the bed and ran to the bathtub. I glanced back at Troy whose mouth was hanging wide open, and his dick was at half-mast.

"So that's how it's gonna be huh, Sunshine?"

"Yes. At least for now," I laughed and turned the water on.

"Think there's room for two in there?" he asked, standing up and stretched. God damn Troy was built. Every time I looked at him, I was in awe that this man wanted to be with me. Well, at least, he wanted me to be in his bed with him. Lord knew if I had made any headway in with a relationship between us. I really wouldn't know if he did want a relationship with me until this whole Banachi fiasco got cleared up. Right now I felt like I was being pushed on him and he had no choice. I didn't want him to feel that he had to be with me.

"What's with the frown, Sunshine?" he asked, walking over to me, his dick bobbing and waving at me.

I pasted a smile on my face. There was no point in telling Troy what I was thinking. "No frown. I was just wondering if two people can fit in the shower and how we only have thirteen minutes left until Meg comes barging in here."

"Then you better get your sexy ass in here with me," Troy said as he walked past me and right into the shower, leaving the curtain open behind him.

Well, what was a girl to do? Stand here and worry about the future, or enjoy the delicious man who was waiting in the shower?

I was wet and totally in the moment five seconds later. Mama didn't raise no fool.

*_*_*_*_*_*_*_*_*

Chapter 19

TROY

"Everyone has their clothes on? All the bits and pieces put away?" Meg asked as she walked in the door, her hand covering her eyes.

"Babe," King laughed as he watched her walk right into the island and grunted.

"I'm not opening my eyes until I have firm confirmation that Troy's ass is fully covered. I can't handle that kind of thing twice in one day." She had turned and was talking to the cabinets.

"Meg, take your damn hand off your face. You think I would walk you into a room where there was a naked guy other than me?" King growled, grabbing her arm and gently lowering it.

"No, I don't think you would." Meg still had her eyes shut tight.

"Meg, I have fucking clothes on," I called, shaking my head as I quickly made the bed.

"Promise?"

"Hell yes."

She opened one eye and slowly turned around, looking around the apartment. "Don't ever do that to me again," she said, one eye still closed and pointed a finger at me.

"Knock, Meg, and if no one answers, wait longer," I laughed.

"Dually noted," she said, opening both eyes. "You might want to invest in a tanning membership by the way. Your ass is unusually pale."

"I might have to agree with Meg on that one," Marley said as she walked out of the stall in the corner.

"You got any beer, brother?" King asked as he opened the fridge and looked around.

"Bottom left." I grabbed the pillow that had ended up on the floor and tossed it at the head of the bed. "Grab me one, too." The beer I had opened earlier sat on the counter forgotten and warm.

"Do you have anything to eat, I'm starving," Meg mumbled as she opened the cabinets looking for food.

"Check the freezer, there should be some snacks in there you can heat up."

"Heck yeah, I'm hungry, too," Marley said as she walked over to Meg and they both peered into the freezer.

"Dude, I think you need to buy stock in pizza rolls. You have like six bags in here," Meg said as she grabbed a bag and tossed it on the counter.

"Oh, popsicles!" Marley grabbed the half-eaten box of twin banana popsicles and pulled one out. "Split one with me?" she asked Meg as she opened it and snapped it in half handing it to me.

"Hell yes."

"After you feed yourselves, you think you can tell me what the hell ya'll are doing here?" I said as I watched Meg grab down a plate and load it up with pizza rolls.

"You didn't invite them over?" Marley asked.

"Hell no. I see Meg enough at work," I smirked, cracking open my beer.

"Ass," Meg said, raising her hand up and flipping me off over her shoulder.

"We need to talk," King said as he sat down on the couch.

I grabbed Marley's hand and tugged her over to the sofa with me. I didn't need Meg's 'uniqueness' wearing off on her. "What's up?" I asked, popping open the footrest.

"Gravel stopped by your house earlier today."

"OK."

"When he got there, your door was kicked in, and your whole house was tossed."

"Oh my God," Marley gasped, her hand covering her mouth.

"Holy shit," I cursed.

"As of right now we are assuming it's the Banachi's. I had to call in a favor from the Chilton chapter to help get in touch with them. As of right now, all they are getting is silence."

"So they are still trying to get to Marley. Are they even going to care when you talk to them and tell them Marley doesn't want the money?"

"We'll make them listen. I have Edge researching everything he can about inheritance law. There had to be a way to refuse the money or accept it and just give it back to his family."

"I tried!" Marley shouted.

"I'm not saying you didn't, Marley. We're just double-checking to make sure you didn't miss anything. Edge has a cousin who is a lawyer, and he pulled a favor in. Hopefully, he'll know something in the next couple of days,"

King said, turning his head to watch Meg in the kitchen. "What the hell are you doing in there, babe?" he called.

"Decorating for Christmas. What the hell do you think I'm doing? I'm hungry." Meg pulled the plate from the microwave and grabbed two sodas and a couple more beers for King and me.

"You always have to sass me?" King asked as he grabbed the drinks out of her hands.

"Don't ask such obvious questions and I won't have to sass you so much." Meg popped a pizza roll in her mouth and smiled at King.

"You know where that sass ends you up," he growled, leaning in and snatched the plate out of her hands.

"Hey!" Meg yelled and grabbed the plate back. "Don't even say it, Lo, or its couch city tonight for you."

"That sass gets a di-" Meg shoved a hand full of pizza rolls in his mouth and flounced over to the other end of the couch and plopped down next to Marley. "Fucking cavemen," Meg mumbled under her breath.

Marley burst out laughing as King wiped pizza sauce off his face and chewed on at least four pizza rolls. His cheeks were bulging out, and he was looking at Meg like he didn't know whether to throttle her or kiss her.

"Pizza roll?" Meg asked, holding the plate out to Marley and me. Marley grabbed two, a smirk playing on her lips. "Sure, don't want you to smash them in my face or anything."

"Your ass is mine as soon as we leave," King growled, finally swallowing down the pizza rolls.

Meg rolled her eyes but wisely didn't say anything.

"You're going to have to stay here until we get things under control. The Banachi's are going to keep looking for you, Marley. As of right now, this is the safest place for you. I didn't even know this place was here until Meg showed it to me," King said, wiping his hands on his jeans.

"Are you sure they didn't follow you here? Who's to say they won't find us here?" Marley said, and I could see the panic start to take her over.

"No one followed us, and I don't know how they could know about this place. You have nothing to worry about here. Crowbar and Turtle should be here within the hour and will be staying up here, too. I figure they can camp out in the garage. You won't even know they are here if you want." King stood up and looked at Meg, who had her mouth full. "You wanna go for a four-wheeler ride with me, babe? I wanna take a look around and check things out."

Meg shook her head no and pointed at me. "Take him. I don't trust being alone with you right now. I can tell the caveman is still front and center."

"God help me," Lo said, shaking his head.

"I'll take ya." I leaned over and kissed Marley on the side of her head. "Be right back, Sunshine," I whispered in her ear.

"OK," she mumbled back, turning her head and quickly kissed me on the lips.

I grabbed my boots out from under the bed and slipped them on. King was already out the door and climbing on the four wheeler Marley had driven before.

"Try to distract him from the punishment he thinks he needs to dole out to me later," Meg called.

"Maybe you need it, Meg," I said, walking out the door.

"Traitor!" she yelled as I shut the door.

I climbed on my four wheeler and looked at King. "She's fucking crazy."

"Yeah, but I wouldn't have it any other way," he gruffed, trying to act like he wasn't wrapped around her finger.

"It's about time I saw her happy. You did that to her." Sappy, but it was the damn truth. No matter how crazy and batty Meg was, she was and always will be one of my best friends. She deserved the happiness that she had found with King.

"I just give her what she deserves, brother. She's the one who gave me a reason to live. Seeing her smile every day lets me know I'm finally doing something right with my life." King cleared his throat and turned his head away. At that moment, I knew how much Meg meant to King.

"Alright, enough sappy shit. Follow me and I'll show you all the trails." I fired up the four-wheeler and took off down the trails. I glanced back seeing King close behind and gunned it, kicking up dust.

As I was walking out the door, I could see the fear creeping back into her eyes. She had the same look on her face when we had been shot at and told me to leave. I wasn't going to let her push me away this time. Running away wasn't going to fix her problems.

She was going to let me help fix them and then her ass wasn't going anywhere except to my bed.

--*-*-*-*-*-*-*-*-*

Chapter 20

Marley

"You need another drink?" Meg asked, walking over to the fridge.

"I didn't even open the first one you gave me." I glanced at the island where Lo had set the two sodas Meg had given him.

"Me neither. I think," Meg opened the cabinet above the sink and pulled down three bottles, "you and I need something stronger than soda right now."

Meg turned back around and grabbed two shot glasses down. "I don't think you could be more right," I said, standing up and sat down on a stool by the island.

"You okay with southern comfort?" she asked as she filled both glasses to the top.

I grabbed mine and took a sniff. "I've never had Southern Comfort."

"Well slap me silly and call me Bernice. I'm about to pop your cherry, darlin'." Meg grabbed hers and clinked it against my glass. "Bottoms up," she toasted and tossed her's back.

I quickly tossed mine back, and my eyes squinted at the sharp taste. "Not bad," I whizzed.

Meg threw her head back and laughed, "You'll get used to it." She filled up our glasses two more times, and I threw them back without hesitation. By the time she filled my glass up for the fourth time, I was starting to relax.

She pushed the glass towards me, but I didn't grab it right away. "Are you trying to get me drunk?"

"Yes. I saw the same look in your eye you had when you proclaimed you were leaving. I needed to distract you. Booze was the fastest way." She clinked her glass against mine and tossed her shot back like it was water.

I threw mine back and felt it burn down my throat. "I think I need to slow down," I mumbled as she lined up our glasses again and filled them. "How the hell are you still standing?" I slurred and leaned over to look at her legs.

Meg put her hand on my shoulder and tilted me back upright in my chair. "I forgot you're not from Wisconsin."

"No. But I like it here." Wait, was that the answer to the question? Did Meg ask me a question?

"Good. But now we need to sober you up before Troy gets back. He's going to piss himself when he finds out I got you hammered." Meg whirled around from the island and started opening up cabinets.

"I'm not hammered," I said, although I think it might have come out hammmm. I'm not sure.

"Of course, you're not, sweetie, I just think some coffee would be a good idea," Meg said as she frantically searched the cabinets. "Lo is going to kill me for this. It's not my fault I'm from Wisconsin and drink most women under the table. It's what we do in the winter to stay warm; drink. And well, have sex. That's why there're so many babies born in August and September. Or at least, that's what I like to think," Meg rambled on as she opened the last cabinet and found the coffeemaker. "Jackpot!"

My head was swimming by the time she had it plugged in and coffee was dripping into the pot. I was still trying to process her ramblings from before. "So this winter I need to drink and have lots of sex?"

"What?" she asked, looking at me like I had grown two heads.

"What you shed before, about this summer, ugh, I mean winter. Yes, winter." Woo, maybe coffee was a good idea. I was struggling to put two words together.

"Um, well I'm sure Troy will be good with the lots of sex, but if this is how you hold your liquor, honey, you might want to stick to wine coolers." Meg leaned against the counter and looked at me.

I was still on my stool, but I was now hunched over and sprawled out on the counter. "Don't judge, my body isss to heapy toooo stay up," I slurred. I closed my eyes and tried to clear my foggy brain. Sweet Jesus, I needed to lie down.

"Coffees ready!" Meg chirped as she grabbed a cup down and filled it. "Drink this, hun. Lo and Troy could be back any second."

She slid the cup towards me and the smell of rich coffee swirled around me. I pulled myself up and wrapped my hands around the cup. "Aren't you going to have some?" I asked as I took a sip.

"No. I'm good, just got a lite buzz. Good thing Lo drove. That pot of coffee is all for you. So you need to drink your ass off." I took three big gulps, and it burned down my throat.

"Put a couple of ice cubes in it. It's too fooking hot now."

"Did you just say fooking?" Meg giggled as she walked over to the freezer and grabbed the ice cube tray out.

"I don't know, it's a fooking possibility," I laughed, dropping an ice cube into my cup. Meg threw her head back laughing hysterically.

"Oh my God, you so have to come out with Cyn and I. It would be fooking hilarious," Meg snorted.

My coffee sloshed over the side of the cup, spilling all over my hand as a fit of laughter bubbled out from me. Meg tossed the towel at me and grabbed the coffee cup.

"Don't spill anymore. If I know Lo, he's not going to be gone for much longer. Drink up," Meg ordered, wiping up the counter.

I dropped another ice cube in my cup and chugged down half. I really did need to sober so Meg didn't get into trouble with King. I think she was in enough trouble with shoving a plate of pizza rolls in his face. I burst out laughing, spewing coffee everywhere, remembering King's head smeared with sauce and cheese.

"Oh...my... King...and the pizza...his face..." I wheezed out. I couldn't stop laughing. King was always so put together and in control that seeing him with food all over his face just cracked me up.

"Ass deserved it," Meg cackled, wiping up the coffee I had just spat out.

"The look on his-." A loud knocking on the door made Meg and I jump. We both stared at the door, but neither of us moved.

"Meg! Open the door, I locked it on the way out," Troy called.

"Shit!" Meg whispered.

"I'm drunk!" I whispered back.

Meg burst out laughing, smothering it with the back of her hand. "I know," she whispers shouted, "Take this and go to the bathroom. I'll try to hold them back." She shoved the coffee pot at me and helped me off the stool.

I stumbled two steps to the bathroom and Meg steadied me. She quickly guided me to the toilet and shut the door behind me. I set the coffee pot on the floor and collapsed onto the closed toilet seat. I heard the clanking of bottles and figured Meg was putting away the evidence.

"Meg!" I heard Troy shout again.

Shit, he did not sound happy. I grabbed the coffee pot, thinking I better get to chugging and realized I forgot my coffee cup. Shit on a brick! How the hell was I supposed to drink this?

I frantically looked around, praying a cup would magically appear but no such luck.

"Where's Marley?" I heard mumbled through the door.

"Shitting," Meg blurted out. I burst out laughing, sloshing the coffee over the top. Apparently, Meg didn't do well under pressure. "Ugh, I mean she's in the bathroom," I heard her mumble.

I slapped my hand over my mouth, hoping Troy didn't hear me.

"So, she's in the bathroom, shitting?" Troy asked. I felt a giggle building up and knew I had to keep it together. I closed my eyes and tried to picture my old English professor giving a lecture to try and calm me down. It worked until Meg opened her mouth again.

"Yes, totally in the bathroom shitting. The best place to shit." I couldn't hold it in anymore. I burst out laughing, throwing my head back and smashed it against the wall.

"Babe, what the hell is going on?" I heard King's low, gravelly voice.

"Nothing. Nothing at all."

I picked up the coffee pot and pried the little cover doohickey off and tossed it on the floor. Just as I had the pot raised to my lips, the bathroom door swung open, and Troy stood on the other side.

"What the fuck?" He asked. I sat there, the coffee pot still raised to my lips, motionless. I had no idea what to say.

"Um, Marley was in the bathroom, and she told me she was thirsty and I, ugh, got her something to drink." Meg chimed in, standing behind Troy.

"So you made her a pot of coffee, brought it to the bathroom, gave it to her without a cup and shut the door?"

"Yes, exactly," Meg said, nodding her head.

"While she was shitting," King laughed from the sofa.

"Shut it, Lo," Meg hissed, crossing her arms over her chest.

"What the hell is going on?" Troy demanded.

"They're drunk, brother," King laughed.

"How the hell did you know that?" Meg yelled and turned to look at King.

"You left the door open to the liquor cabinet, babe."

Troy, Meg and I each looked into the kitchen and saw the door wide open. "Son of a bitch!" Meg cursed.

"What the hell were you doing drinking? And how the hell did you get drunk, we were only gone for half an hour," Troy asked. I couldn't tell if he was pissed or amazed Meg and I had managed to get drunk so quickly.

"First off, I'm not drunk," Meg said, resting her hands on her hips. "Second, I was just trying to help you out, Troy."

King burst out laughing, throwing his arms in the air. "You were only helping. Lord help us if Meg's way of helping is getting drunk," King said, laughing his ass off.

Meg gave him the stink eye and flipped him off which only made him laugh even harder. "If you'll ignore the laughing hyena on the couch, I'll explain."

"This ought to be good," King mumbled under his breath.

Meg ignored King and continued on, "Marley had the deer in the headlights look when you left, and I knew she was freaking out. I figured a shot would help relax her."

"You got wasted off one shot?" Troy's eye shot to me, shocked.

"No!" Meg yelled. "She's a definite lightweight but not that bad. I kind of lost count, but I think we did five or so."

"Of what?" Troy demanded.

"Sormn cmfegt," Meg said, wiping her mouth with the back of her hand as she talked.

"What?" Troy asked, confused.

"It's Meg, brother. She gave her shots of Southern Comfort," King called from the couch as he flipped the TV on.

"Hey, you say that like I'm predictable!" Meg sassed at King. He just shook his head and started flipping channels.

"I still don't understand how Marley ended up in the bathroom with a pot of coffee," Troy said, glancing at the pot I still had in my hands.

"Don't be mad at Meg, please," I pleaded, shuffling over to the island and set the coffee pot down. "This wasn't any of her fault. I didn't know how strong Southern Comfort was. She didn't force me to take the shots."

"I'm not mad, I just don't understand what the hell happened in the thirty minutes I was gone."

"OK, I'll explain." Troy stared at me, waiting. "So, I was ready to run, like get the hell out of dodge. Somehow Meg knew before I even said anything."

"I know. I saw the look in your eyes before I left."

"See, I freaking helped!" Meg yelled, throwing her hands up in the air. She stomped over to the couch and collapsed into King's lap.

"Getting her drunk was your bright idea? I'm sure there was something else you could have done. Maybe *talk* to her?!" Troy shouted at Meg.

"We're fucked. Anything serious happens, Meg is going to get everyone drunk, and Marley is going to get the fuck out of dodge." King stood up, grabbing Meg and threw his empty beer can in the garbage.

"Hey, at least, she didn't run. Now she's mellow and complacent, you should be thanking me." Meg pulled out of Kings arms and grabbed the coffee pot, dumping what was left down the drain.

"Let's go, babe, we got some talking to do about your coping skills. Opening a bottle is not always the right answer," King laughed, pulling his sunglasses off the top of his head and pushed them onto his nose.

"It worked. Don't go all caveman on me, Lo." Meg wagged her finger at King and set the coffee pot back under the machine.

"You got me there, babe, it definitely worked," Lo laughed, holding the door open for her.

"We'll leave your bags by the front door. Let Lo know if you need anything more, Marley, and I'll see about getting it to you." Meg waved and walked out the door, slugging King in his gut as she walked by.

King grunted and grabbed her and swung her up into his arms. She squealed and cussed as the door shut behind them.

I looked at Troy, who was staring at the shut door and wondered what the hell he was thinking. He didn't seem terribly upset, although he could have been keeping his cool with Meg and King around.

"Um, I'm sorry about the whole drinking thing. Meg and I were just talking, and it sort of happened," I said, chewing on my lip.

"That seems to happen a lot when Meg is around. Hell, I've been involved in half of the things that just happen when she is around," Troy laughed, running his fingers through his hair.

"Are you mad?" I asked, afraid of the answer.

"Oh, Sunshine. You've got a lot to learn about me, just like I have a lot to learn about you. I'm not mad, at least not at you."

"Don't be mad at Meg, either."

"I'm not mad at her. I'm fucking pissed at your fucking ex's family. This shit is getting so fucking ridiculous. You didn't ask for any of this, but they are still acting like you stole their family fortune right from under their noses." Troy walked over to me and wrapped his arms around me and pulled me close.

"I'm sorry you have to deal with this. I can go if you want. I'm sure you don't want to be held captive for God knows how long with me here," I whispered.

"You're not going anywhere, Marley. I don't know how many times I'm going to have to tell you that, but I'm going to tell you every day until you get it through that pretty little head of yours. You can't fix this on your own. Hell, I can't even fix it all by myself. We both need King and the Knights to help. They have connections to things that I wouldn't even know where to begin. Just let us help." He rubbed my back, making me relax into his arms.

"I'm scared, Troy. I don't know what to do," I whispered.

"For right now, you do nothing. Sit on the stool and I'll make our dinner." He pressed a kiss to the top of my head and pulled me over to the stool.

"What did King have to say while you guys were outside?"

Troy opened the freezer and pulled out a bag of french fries and some frozen hamburger patties. "He thinks once they get in touch with the Banachi's that they will get everything squared away, but until then we need to lay low. He said this is the safest place for us. When I'm at work, you'll be here with at least two guys from the club until I get home."

"They're going to be here even when you are, right? I think the more people we have here watching the better."

"You think I can't protect you, Sunshine?" Troy asked as he grabbed a contraption out of one of the cupboards and put it on the counter.

"Yes, I mean no, but yes."

Troy threw his head back and laughed. "Make up your mind, Sunshine, you're killing my ego right now."

"No, no no," I shook my head. "I didn't mean you can't take care of me. I just meant you can take care of me, but I don't want you to." Troy looked at me like I was absolutely insane. I guess I didn't clear that up any better.

"Does that mean you want Crowbar and Demon to come in here and make your dinner?"

"No!" Hell no. I was totally botching explaining this. "I mean you stay here, with me, and they can be out there taking care of whatever. I don't want you out there with whatever." I don't think that was a better explanation. I blame the Southern Comfort. My brain was apparently a bit foggy still.

"I think I got you, Sunshine, although you might want to try and explain that to me tomorrow when you're not so blitzed." Troy poured oil into the machine he had grabbed from the cabinet and dropped a metal basket into it.

"That's a deep fryer," I said, realizing what it was.

"Uh, yeah." Troy grabbed a pan and held it up. "And this is a frying pan."

"You're an ass," I laughed and tossed the wet towel on the counter at him. He grabbed it out of the air and tossed it over his shoulder.

"Cat like reflexes, baby." he smirked.

"Still an ass."

"Let's not forget it's an ass you like," he winked at me.

Oh jeez, how could I forget that conversation? "I plead the fifth."

"I'll have you pleading anything but the fifth tonight, Sunshine."

"Oh really? Is that a threat?"

"No, that's a promise you can take to the bank, Sunshine. I never make a promise I don't intend to keep."

Troy turned back to the fryer and finished dumping the oil in. I watched him as he cooked dinner, noticing how his shirt stretched taut across his shoulders when he reached up in a cupboard. How snug his ass was in his jeans and that each time he bent over I swear my heartbeat speed up, and the room got ten degrees hotter.

By the time he had the burgers sizzling on the griddle, and the fries were dropped into the oil, my mouth was watering, and I was starving for more than food.

--*-*-*-*-*-*-*

Chapter 21

TROY

Marley was laid out on the couch, one hand holding her stomach and wagging a finger at me. "I can't believe you made me eat two burgers and all those fries. You're such an ass."

"I think you're starting to give me a complex with how many times you call me an ass," I laughed, grabbing her plate off the coffee table and headed into the kitchen.

"You don't really think that I think that, do you?" she called as I rinsed off the plates and stuck them in the dishwasher.

I shook my head and laughed. Marley really did have a lot to learn about me. I tended to take everything as a joke and rarely got upset. I called her Sunshine, and I guess she called me Ass. "As much as I'd like to mess with you right now, seeing as you're still a little tipsy, but no, baby, I don't think you mean it."

"Mmm, good," she mumbled from the couch.

I finished cleaning up the kitchen, flipping off all the lights and headed back to the living room. Crow and Ham had shown up right as I was dropping the fries into the fryer and I had wound up making dinner for them also. They had taken their food and headed back to the garage though to keep an eye out. They had said they had brought a couple of cots and blankets and should be fine in the garage, even though it had been getting rather cold at night.

"I'm gonna grab a drink, Sunshine, you want one, have you had enough?"

"Uh, drink yes, shot, hell no," she groaned from the couch.

"How about an Old Fashioned. For your first time trying Southern, Meg should have made you an Old Fashioned, not shots," I said, shaking my head as I grabbed the substantially lighter bottle down. Meg and Marley really put a dent in the bottle I had just opened.

"It tasted good, it just knocked me on my ass," she giggled from the couch.

"Well, I can promise I'm not trying to knock you on your ass."

"More like get into my ass."

I threw my head back laughing and held onto the counter. "Jesus Christ, baby,... did you hear... what you just... said?" I wheezed out.

"You know what I meant," Marley mumbled from the couch. "You're just trying to get in my pants. Let me tell you, you're a shoe-in. No need to get me hammered."

"Good to know," I said, shaking my head as I grabbed two glasses down from the cabinet and set them next to the bottle of Southern. I pushed one glass aside, deciding to make just one drink we could share.

"How long do you think it's going to take to get things back to normal?"

I grabbed a can of lemon-lime soda out of the fridge and a couple of ice cubes. "Hopefully not too long. I think it's just a matter of getting in touch with the Banachi's and explaining things."

"Hmm, I hope you're right. I'm assuming I can't go to work?"

"No, Sunshine," I called, filling up the glass and headed into the living room.

"Damn, I should probably call Gwen. She's going to freak when she finds out. She's been looking for another stylist, but hasn't found one yet." Marley leaned off the couch, reaching for her cell phone that was on the coffee table.

I grabbed her phone and tossed it on the other end of the couch. "No phone calls right now."

"Hey, why the hell not. She's going to wonder where the hell I am when I don't show up to work." Marley pouted, laying back down.

"King said he was sending Gambler over there to let her know. Don't worry about it. You can call her tomorrow if you really want to," I said, sitting down by her feet.

She sat up and shot daggers at me with her pissed off stare. "Why the hell can't I call her now?" She demanded.

"Because tonight all the bullshit with your ex and the Banachi's doesn't exist. It's just you and me. You need a night to relax and not worry."

"What if something happens? How the hell are we supposed to know?"

"I told King to call the house phone if he needed anything."

"You have a house phone? Who the hell has one of those anymore? I thought everyone had cell phones?" Marley asked, amazed.

I shook my head and kicked my feet up on the coffee table. Marley was a nut. I know a lot of people only did have cell phones, but there were still some of us that held onto the past. "I guess I'm the one person who still has one."

"So what if the house phone doesn't ring, then what?" she asked, sitting up.

"Then nothing is wrong."

"But what if there is something wrong, but your house phone isn't working, and we don't know it. What the hell are we supposed to do?"

Jesus Christ, the whole point of the no phones tonight was to help Marley relax, but it seemed to be having the opposite effect on her. "It's working, Sunshine. Now get your ass over here and help me pick out a movie." She needed to stop worrying and chill.

"I'm right here," she said, looking at me.

"No, Sunshine, you are about four feet away from me. I want you. Right. Here." I pointed to my lap.

Her eyes went wide, and I think she finally figured out what I mean. She crawled over to me and straddled my lap. Much better.

"Is this what you wanted?" She asked, grabbing the drink out of my hand and took a sip.

"It'd be better if we didn't have any clothes on, but we'll get there," I whispered, grabbing the drink out of her hand and wrapped my arm around her. I leaned forward, her body pressed against me and set the glass on the coffee table. She tried to scoot backward, but I held her tight. "No running away, Marley," I whispered, brushing her hair from her neck and nuzzled her ear.

"I'm not running... I just trying... to um..." she trailed off as I slid a hand under her shirt and stroked her back. She rested her arms on my shoulders and tilted her head to the left, and I trailed kisses down her neck.

"I've never tasted anything sweeter than you, Marley. You drive me crazy night and day. All I want is to lock you in my room and never let you out." I flipped her over onto the couch, her soft, luscious body laid out beneath me.

"You do the same thing to me, Troy. I can't go five minutes without thinking about you," she moaned, stretching her arms over her head. I reached down, grabbing the bottom of her shirt and pulled it up, exposing her smooth skin and breasts incased in her blood red bra. The color red had never driven me crazy before, but now I knew every time I saw the color red I would think of Marley and her soft curves that drove me crazy.

I pulled the shirt up over her head and tossed it onto the floor. I needed to see all of her again. It had only been a couple of hours since I had taken her, but I needed her again. I reached down, popping open the button of her jeans and slid the zipper down. She arched her hips up, giving me the silent permission I needed to pull her jeans off.

I shimmied her jeans off, down her perfect ass and curvy legs. "I don't know how you do it, Marley. You're like food to a starving man. All I want to do is devour you and never surface," I growled.

Her body trembled at my words, and a moan escaped her lips. "Troy."

"Shh, I'm right here, baby. I know you need the same thing I need." I grabbed the waistband of her panties and pulled them down and off her legs.

I leaned down, inhaling her intoxicating scent and buried my tongue into her perfect pussy. I flicked her clit and her hips bucked, begging for more. She spread her legs wide, giving me all the access I needed to drive her insane.

I stuck a finger in her greedy little hole and felt a tremor take over her body again. I rocked my finger in and out of her as my tongue worked over her clit, bringing her closer and closer to the edge.

"Troy," she screamed out as I added another finger and pounded into her. She gripped the couch cushion and pressed her sweet pussy into my mouth, needing more.

"I'm gonna cum, I'm gonna cum," she chanted over and over.

I sucked her clit into mouth, flicking it with the tip of my tongue, and she exploded around me. "Troy," she gasped as her body quaked around me, ecstasy taking her over.

I released her clit, giving it one last flick and she moaned. The sounds of her cries and moans went straight to my dick, and I needed her right then.

I pulled back from her body, popped open the button on my jeans and quickly stripped them off. I yanked my boxers halfway off and plunged into her. I couldn't wait.

She grabbed onto my shoulders, pulling herself up and dug her fingernails into my back. She tossed her head back as I pulled out and slammed back into her. Her drenched pussy gripped my dick and milked it.

"You're mine, Marley," I grunted, grabbing her hips and pounded into her.

"Yes, God yes, take me, Troy," Marley moaned.

I looked down at her as she took her arms off my shoulders and pushed her bra up, showing me her perfect tits. She pinched her hard nipples and wrapped her legs around my waist. God dammit, Marley was a fucking goddess.

"Fuck me, I can't wait much more." I groaned, clenching my eyes shut, trying not to cum.

"Cum. Cum for me, Troy," Marley pleaded, clenching her already tight pussy around my dick.

I collapsed on top of her, my fists clenching the cushion as I rocked in and out, giving her everything I had. I gave one final stroke, and I couldn't hold it back anymore. I exploded inside her while her mumbled pleas and moans surrounded me.

Marley ran her fingers through my hair, and I buried my face in her neck. "Can we do that again?" she giggled.

All I could muster up was a smile, and I shook my head no. Marley had just completely wrung me out, and she was ready for round two. Definitely a wildcat.

"Give me a couple of hours, Sunshine. I might need to lay here for a couple of minutes before I even think about getting up."

"Well, you might have to get up sooner than that. I can feel you dripping down my leg, and I don't want to get it on your couch."

"Don't worry-." I started, but then it sunk in what Marley had just said. I was about to start dripping down her leg. Son of a bitch! I forgot a condom.

I pulled out of her, my dick protesting leaving its soft, warm cocoon. I pushed off the couch to get off of her, but she wouldn't let go.

"Marley, let me go. I forgot the condom," I ranted, reaching around my back to grab her arms.

"Troy, stop."

"What? No, let me go," I had never had sex without a condom on. I wanted to have kids someday, but today was not that day.

"Troy, I'm on the pill."

"I can't believe I let this happen. I'm so sorry, baby. If anything happens, I promise I'll be there for you and the baby. I'd never leave you or our baby." I managed to pry her arms from around me and pulled her up so she was sitting.

"Troy, did you hear what I said?" she asked.

"Yes, I'm dripping down your leg. Come on, up. I'll clean you up." I grabbed her wrist and stood up, pulling her up behind me.

She yanked her arm out of my hold and crossed her arms over her chest. "Troy, listen to me."

"Marley, can we talk later. We need to get you cleaned up, and then you need to rest." Pregnant women needed lots of rest, right? Shower and then she was going to bed.

"Troy!" Marley shouted, yanking me from my thoughts of getting her to bed. "I'm on the fucking pill!"

"That's good, Marley, but now we-" Wait, did she just say she's on the pill? "You're on the pill?"

"Yes, for the third time, I'm on the pill! Good God, I swear you were five minutes away from naming our firstborn. I'm on the pill, we should be fine." She reached out and grabbed my hand. "Although that shower sounds like a good idea, I do have plans for something more than sleeping after," she purred, pulling me towards the shower.

"Wait," I said, tugging on her arm to stop. She turned around, and it looked like she was ready to hit me over the head with a baseball bat.

"Yes?"

"I'm clean." She looked at me like I was crazy.

"Well, I'm not." She stepped back and pointed to her thighs that had my cum dripping down them.

Son of a bitch, that was sexy to see my cum dripping from her sweet pussy. I shook my head, trying to stay focused. "No, not that. I meant I'm clean as in I've been checked out, and I've never been with anyone but you without a condom."

"Oh, OK. Good. I'm clean, too," she whispered, ducking her head down.

"What's wrong, baby?" I asked, reaching for her chin and tilting her head up.

"You're not the first I've been with without a...." she trailed off, not finishing her sentence.

Shit. Her fiancée, of course. "Have you been tested since then?"

"Of course! I would never have let you do that if there might have been a chance. It was only with Mark and it wasn't all the time." She blushed bright red, and she looked back down at the floor.

Not exactly the thing I want to be thinking about with my dick hanging out, but there was no reason my Marley had to feel bad about it. "Look at me, Marley." She shook her head no and took a step back to run away. "Not so fast, Sunshine." I grabbed her hand before she had a chance to get away and pulled her to me. "Don't run from me. I'm not mad. You had a life before me, baby. I can't get upset about that. Do I want to hear about it word for word? Hell no. You telling me what you just did was something you needed to tell me. I'm ok with that," I grabbed her chin again and tilted her head up. "Don't run from me, Marley. You promised you wouldn't do that anymore."

A lone tear fell from her eyes, and I wiped it away. "I'm sorry. I try not to run, but it's hard not to sometimes."

"Try harder, baby. I promise there is nothing you can tell me that will make me turn away from you. We might have just met and barely know one another, but I know I want you by me. Whether it be at my house, truck, or my bed, I want you there."

Another tear fell from her eye. "I don't deserve what you are willing to give me, Troy. I haven't done anything to deserve it."

"Is that what you think? That you have to give something to get something in return?"

"That's life, Troy."

"Sunshine, you have given me more in the past week or however many days I've known you than all the girls I have ever dated combined."

"I keep running from you."

"So, that's something we need to work on. That doesn't mean I shouldn't treat you good."

"I've never had that before, Troy. Even with my mom, I knew if I messed up or did something wrong, she was going to be pissed at me. Punish me for it for weeks." Tears were streaming down her face, and there was no way I could stop them all.

Standing in the middle of my living room with both of us half naked was not how I wanted us to have this conversation. "Take your bra off, baby." I walked over to the bathtub and turned the water on. I pushed the curtain back so it was in the back and reached under the sink. I pulled out a bottle of shampoo and figured it would do in a pinch for a bath.

I pulled my shirt over my head and tossed it over by the bed. Marley walked over to me, and I grabbed her hand. We silently watched the tub fill, neither of us talking. When the water was halfway up the tub, I opened the shampoo and squirted some into the running water.

"Did you just make me a bubble bath with shampoo?" Marley smirked as I shut the water off.

"No, I made *us* a bubble bath with shampoo." I grabbed her hand and pulled her to me.

"I take we're done talking?" she whispered.

"No, baby, we're just getting started." I stepped into the tub, sinking down under the bubbles.

She laughed as the water splashed and rolled over the side of the tub. "You think there's room in there for me with all those bubbles?"

"This is my first bubble bath in over twenty-five years. Forgive me if my water to soap ratio is off."

She stepped into the tub between my legs and sank down, my legs cradling her. "You're forgiven. It's the thought that counts, handsome," she purred as the bubbles enveloped her.

She leaned back into my chest and stretched her legs out. "I think I like you calling me handsome more than ass."

"Hmm, I'll have to try and remember that."

I grabbed the washcloth I had hanging over the side of the tub and started running it over her body. She moaned as I grazed over her sweet pussy and perfect tits. "We need to finish our talk, baby."

"Fine," Marley mumbled.

"Why do you keep running from me, Sunshine? What happened to you to make you think the best solution is to always run?"

She pulled away from me and turned sideways and looked at me. I could tell she was afraid to tell me, but I wasn't going anywhere until she told me. I needed to know.

--*-*-*-*-*-*-*-*-*

Chapter 22

Marley

"I don't have some sad sob story, Troy. Nothing horrible happened to me, it's just the way I am." This wasn't where I thought our evening would wind up. Granted soaking in the tub with Troy was not something I would bat an eyelash at. Our topic of conversation was less than desirable, though.

"So you've always run away from things that scare you? I doubt that because you were about to be married and would be married right now had it not been for your ex's death."

"I wasn't scared of marrying Mark. I wasn't scared at all when I was with Mark."

"Because you felt safe with him."

I stared at Troy and tried to figure out if that was why I wasn't afraid or running away when I was with Mark. It wasn't that he made me feel safe, it was more like he didn't really make me feel anything. I know that sounds horrible, but that's how it was. If I really was honest with myself, Mark was my best friend, and I loved him, but it wasn't the kind of love you had for someone you married. "I guess I was safe with Mark. There wasn't much danger or well, anything to worry about. He worked a lot and so did I."

"So at the first sign of danger, you ran to your dad. If Mark would have been alive and you needed help, would you have turned to him?"

"Uh, if it had to do with business I guess I would have, but if it had to deal with the Banachi's or anything like that, then no."

"Could he protect you?"

Mark protect me? That was a good question. Mark worked out three times a week and ran, but I don't think he would have the physical strength to protect me, let alone know what to do. He did always have his driver, Mo, nearby who, from the looks of him, could more than defend me if the need were to arise. "I don't see what this has to do with me running."

"I'm trying to understand you, Sunshine. You don't need to get all sassy with me."

"Sorry, but I just don't know why we have to dissect the relationship I had with Mark. He helped when I needed it with my mom. He was there for me. I owed him a lot for that."

"So marrying him was your way of thanking him?"

"What?! That is not why I was going to marry him. He was a good guy with a good head on his shoulders, and he was going places."

"Sounds rather boring."

"I repeat, what does this have to do with me running?" I was about to lose it if Troy didn't tell me what the hell he was trying to get at.

"You ran from your mother, baby, right into Mark. Then you stayed because it was safe and nothing scared you."

"So, it was the logical thing to do. Why the hell would I want to be with someone who scared me and made me want to run?"

"Then what are you doing here, baby. You told me multiple times you're scared."

"Because, well, because…" Shit, why the hell did I stay? Besides, from the fact always got talked into staying, what made me stay? "You make the scary shit not so scary."

"Why, baby?"

Because he was strong yet sweet, rough and tough yet kind. He made me feel like I was wanted. Even that first night we were together when we barely knew each other, he made me feel like he wanted me to be there. Troy made me feel things I never thought I could. He made me feel wanted and safe while still letting me be myself. "You make me feel safe. You make me wish I had never moved to California and met Mark."

"I'm glad you had Mark, Sunshine. He was there to help you when I couldn't be. He may have not been the right man for you, but he kept you safe for me until I could find you."

"You can't mean that, Troy. We barely know each other."

"I never say something I don't mean, baby. You need to remember that. I know we have a long way to go to getting to know one another, but I think you need to know that I want you here, and I don't want you to leave." He leaned forward, kissing me lightly on the lips and leaned back in the tub.

What do I say to that? What do I do? Mark never said those words to me, and we were going to get married. Maybe Troy was right. I had run to Mark to escape my mom, and I stayed because everything else was too scary or different. But now I didn't have that. Troy was so different from Mark. Mark was straight-laced, lived for his job and barely ever laughed.

Troy worked, but it wasn't like all he thought about was his job. He laughed all the time and was one of the most laid back people I had ever met. He made me happy just by laying on the couch and watching a movie with me. I had never been as happy as I had been the past two weeks. "I don't want to go anywhere, Troy."

"Then don't, baby girl." Troy held his hand out to me. I stared down at it and knew if I took his hand, I was taking a huge step. But if I didn't take his hand, I was taking a huge step away from him. "I might try to run again," I whispered.

"Do you want me to stop you?"

"Yes," I grabbed his hand, and he pulled me to him. I straddled his hips and wrapped my arms around his neck. I had just made one of the most terrifying decisions of my life, but I had never felt safer.

--*-*-*-*-*-*-*-*-*

Chapter 23

Marley

6 days. 144 hours. 8,640 minutes. Don't ask me how many seconds, I'm not that good at math.

Two days ago King told us he had finally gotten in touch with the Banachi's, and they were working things out. He had a meeting with them today, and I was on pins and needles waiting to hear what happened.

"Sunshine, come watch the movie. You staring at the phone on the wall isn't going to make it ring," Troy called from the couch.

I glanced one more time at the phone and trudged over to Troy. "I just want to know what is going on. I should know since it's about me," I pouted, crossing my arms over my chest.

"Marley, we've gone over and over this. Just let King take care of it." He was right. He had told me, at least, three times a day to chill out and leave everything to King. I couldn't stop worrying, though.

"I know, it's just that we don't have much to do, so all I can think about is what's going on. I need a distraction." I was whining, but god damn it I was going stir crazy.

"There's plenty to do."

"Like what? We've done everything there is to do fifty times. I swear if we go for another four wheeler ride, I'm driving till I find civilization."

"Remind me to hide the keys to the four wheelers," Troy mumbled under his breath.

"Ha ha," I flipped Troy off and grabbed the remote that was sitting next to him on the couch. "I get to pick the movie."

I flipped through the channels trying to find something to watch and contemplated chucking the remote at the TV when Troy wrapped his arms around me and tugged me into his lap.

"You've picked the last three movies, I think it's my turn to pick one, Sunshine," Troy rumbled in my ear.

"Oh really?"

"Yes, now hand it over and no one gets hurt." I held the remote up over my head and twisted around to straddle Troy's lap.

"You gonna play dirty again, baby girl?"

"I've been known to," I purred tossing the remote across the room and onto the bed.

"Nice throw but all I have to do is move you off my lap and beat you to the bed. Not a well thought out plan." Troy grabbed my arms and held them behind my back with his hand. My breasts were thrust up in his face and my back arched.

This is what happened at least twice a day. One of us (mostly me) would get restless, and we'd somehow end up sprawled out on the bed or couch working out the tension. There was the one time when we were in the kitchen, and we didn't make it to the couch or the bed. We broke in Troy's island that day.

"You're wearing too many clothes, Marley," Troy growled, grabbing the hem of my shirt and pulling it up. He leaned forward, his lips brushing against the swell of my breasts and I tossed my head back, already on the brink of cumming from just one touch from Troy. I didn't know sex could be like this. Exciting and mind-blowing every time.

"Then take them off, Troy," I purred, grinding my hips into him. He grabbed the cup of my bra and tugged. My breast popped out, and I leaned into Troy, begging for more.

He sucked my nipple into his mouth, and I tugged on my arms, trying to break the hold he had. "Not letting you go, baby girl. I'm gonna lay you out on my bed and feast on you." I moaned low in the back of my throat and stopped trying to get away. Troy having his way with me sounded like a perfect way to release the tension.

"Shit," Troy growled, releasing my tit and sat back letting go of my arms.

"What? What are you doing?" I reached for Troy's neck and pulled him to me. "Don't stop,"

"Sunshine, the door." What? The door? I hadn't heard anyone at the door.

"Open this fucking door or I'm going to kick it in! I haven't seen my daughter in over a week since you kidnapped her!" Gravel was here. Dammit.

"Please tell me you have the door locked." I pulled my bra back up and tugged my shirt down. Gravel yelling at the door was a definite mood killer.

"Hell yes. I learned from Meg walking in on us."

I scooted off Troy's lap and stood up. I looked down at his crotch and saw he still had an impressive boner. "Can't you put that away? My dad is that door," I giggled.

"Yeah, not as easy as you would think. You being in the same room makes me sport a chubby." Troy adjusted himself, trying to disguise his bulge.

"Here, let me help." I reached for Troy's dick, but he batted my hand away.

"Baby, you really think if you touch my dick it'll go down? You touch it, Gravel isn't coming in for at least twenty minutes." Troy shook his head at me and stood up. He threaded his fingers through my hair and brushed his lips against mine. "We'll finish this later," he promised.

"Hmm, we'll see. Gravel might be here to castrate you since you kidnapped me."

"You'll protect me," Troy winked at me. He walked to the door, unlocked it and opened it to a pissed off Gravel.

"About fucking time, Cowboy. Five more seconds and I was going to kick the fucker down," Gravel growled walking past Troy, bumping him with his shoulder.

Troy's eyes flared with rage as Gravel bumped him and his fists clenched. Oh boy. This was going to be interesting.

"Excuse him, Troy. He's been a bear the past week." Ethel walked in behind Gravel and shut the door. "He's been chomping at the bit to come over here all week. I've managed to hold him back this long, but he wasn't listening today. Sorry, we didn't call first," Ethel shut the door behind her and walked over to the kitchen island, setting three plastic grocery bags down.

"No damn reason I should have to call and ask to see my daughter. She should be staying with me right now anyway. Not some cowboy," Gravel huffed as he sat down on the couch, grabbed the remote and started flipping channels.

I looked from Gravel to Troy and shook my head. I swear I was in the twilight zone right now.

185

"Don't you think you should say hi to your daughter since you're finally here?" Ethel scolded.

Gravel turned his gaze to me and wink, "Hey, darlin'," he grunted.

"How about you say hi to the guy whose house you just barged in on?" I shot back.

"Eh." Gravel turned back to the TV and continued to flip channels.

"I'm gonna go for a ride to my house and grab some things since you guys are here," Troy said as he grabbed his truck keys off the top of the fridge. He walked over to the bed where he had his cowboy boots tucked under and pulled them on.

Wait, what? Troy was leaving? "You're leaving?" I asked, panicked.

"Yeah, baby. I'll be back in an hour."

"Can I come with?" I didn't want Troy to leave. I have been with him for the past week and the thought of him leaving left me feeling lost.

"You aren't going anywhere. King still hasn't gotten shit squared away with the Banachi's," Gravel ordered.

"No more than an hour, I promise."

"OK," I whispered, still not liking the idea of Troy leaving.

"Walk me to my truck, Sunshine," Troy called, opening the door.

I raced over to the door, sliding my sandals on and shot out the door.

"Where's the fire, baby girl?" Troy called as he shut the door and followed me around the garage and to his truck.

I leaned up against his truck and waited for him to make it to me. He stood in front of me and shoved his hands in his pockets. "You really need to grab stuff from your house or are you just trying to get away from me?"

"Honestly, Sunshine?" I nodded my head and waited. "I'm pretty sure if I have to spend one more minute with your dad, I'm going to knock his fucking lights out, and I don't want to do that to Ethel."

I pushed off his truck and wrapped my arms around his waist. "Thank God. I thought you were for sure getting the hell out of dodge and not coming back. Although, thank you for not hitting Gravel. I know he means well."

"He needs to get over the bullshit he has swirling around in his head about me."

"Why doesn't he like you? I mean, I know most fathers give their daughter's boyfriends hell, but he seems to have a deeper affliction to you."

"You haven't heard?" he asked, a smirk on his lips.

"Not a clue, tell me."

"He thinks I'm after Meg and just biding my time to swoop in and steal her away from King."

I was speechless. Troy in love with Meg? All you had to do was spend five minutes with them together, and you could see they are only friends. Hell, they could probably pass for brother and sister. "You're shitting me."

"No, Sunshine. He is convinced that a guy and a girl can't be friends without there something going on." Troy reached up and brushed my hair behind my ear.

"For the record, I have never thought you two were more than friends. Meg is head over heels in love with King. You'd have to be blind not to see it."

"Thank God. Another person on my side. I've talked to King about it, and he just laughed his ass off. He said Gravel had talked to him about it before, and he wasn't worried."

"So, my dad didn't like you before, and now that you are dating his daughter, he hates you even more. I don't know if he'll ever like you," I laughed.

"As long as you like me, Sunshine, that's all that matters." He leaned in and brushed his lips against mine.

"I'm pretty sure I like you," I whispered, leaning into his kiss.

"Well, as long as you're pretty sure," he smiled. His lips caressed mine, as he wrapped his arms around me and pushed me into the side up of truck.

"Don't leave. We'll make them leave," I pleaded as he trailed sweet kisses down my neck.

"Hang out with Ethel for a little bit, baby girl. From the looks of her bags she brought, it looks like they are staying for dinner."

I sighed as his hands trailed down my sides and he grabbed my ass, our bodies flush. I delved my fingers into his hair and gripped his head as his kisses rained over my breasts. I arched my chest into him, begging for more.

"Marley!"

Troy stopped kissing me and buried his face in my neck. "Your dad is such a cock blocker," Troy mumbled.

"I'll be right there, Gravel," I hollered back. "He really does have the worst timing," I whined.

"All right, I'm going to run to my house. Is there anything you need from your house? I can stop and get it for you?" Troy leaned back, his eyes connecting with mine.

His eyes were still cloudy with desire, and I could tell he was ten seconds away from throwing me in the back of his truck and having his way with me. "Um, a sweatshirt? Maybe we can have a fire tonight?"

"OK, baby girl. I'll stop by your house and grab some warm clothes. Sure there isn't anything else you need?"

"Nope, the only thing I need is for you to hurry your ass up and get back here."

Troy grabbed me by my neck and laid one on me. I'm talking kissed me so good all thought left me, and all I could do is feel. I held on and just enjoyed the ride.

"Fifty-nine minutes and I'll be back. Maybe less," he growled.

"Make it less," I moaned, kissing him one last time.

Troy stepped back from me and ran his fingers through his hair. "You have no idea how tempted I am to take you with me and drive the hell away from here."

"I think I have a bit of an idea how you feel."

"Stop looking at me like that, Marley. We both know we can't do that. Go help Ethel make dinner, and I promise every dirty little thought that is going through that pretty little head of yours will come true tonight." Troy walked around to the driver's door and climbed in, slamming the door shut behind him.

I moved away from the truck, and he cranked it up. He stuck his hand out the window as he drove away, giving me the typical two fingered guy wave. I watched his truck disappear until I couldn't see the taillights anymore.

"He'll be right back, darlin'. I could see the way that boy was wrapped around your finger as soon as I walked in the door."

I turned around and saw Ethel standing by the corner of the garage. "I like him, Ethel."

"Good, hun. You both need each other."

"I don't know about Troy needing me and all my drama, but I do need him. I've never been with someone who makes me feel the way he does."

"Hold on tight then and don't let go."

This was why I loved Ethel. She always knew the right thing to say. "Did Gravel send you out here to check on me?"

"Oh Lord no. It was more like I had to beat him back from the door. I told him I would see what was holding you up. I knew you were saying goodbye to Troy and didn't need your father breathing down your neck."

"Thanks, Ethel."

"No thanks needed, hun. Now, why don't you go on in the house with me and help me make an apple pie for dinner."

I threw my head back and laughed. "Troy was right. He said you probably brought dinner with you."

"Well of course. I do have manners. I brought all the fixings for meatloaf with all the sides."

I turned my nose up at meatloaf. I had never met a meatloaf I liked. "Ugh, do you think we could maybe have burgers instead of meatloaf?"

Ethel laughed and shook her head. "How about you give my meatloaf a chance and then if you don't like it, I'll make you a hamburger."

"OK, deal."

Ethel headed back to the house, and I followed behind. I glanced behind me, looking where Troy's truck was and smiled. Fifty minutes until he was back.

--*-*-*-*-*-*-*-*

Chapter 24

TROY

My bag was sitting by the door, and I was ready, but I wasn't ready.

I didn't know what the hell I was doing. I didn't understand how I could have such strong feelings for Marley, and I had barely known her. And now I sounded like a wuss. Fuck me, what the hell was Marley doing to me.

I sat down on the couch and ran my fingers through my hair. I always told myself I wanted to settle down and have a family, but I didn't know how it would happen. I never expected a girl to storm into my life and completely take me by surprise.

Looking around my house, everything looked the same, but it didn't feel the same. My whole life looked the same, but damn if it felt the same. I had always valued my time alone. Even when I would date a girl, I would need my own time. I craved it.

With Marley, if she wasn't within ten feet of me I couldn't breathe. I always had to know where she was, and if it weren't next to me, I'd go to her.

The big question was, did she feel the same? Could she breathe without me? I was only her second relationship. Her first relationship had lasted over ten years and, from the sounds of it, had led a sheltered life. Hell, a sheltered and much more expensive life than I could give her. I'm sure Mark had given her everything she needed or wanted.

All I could give Marley she had seen. I worked forty hours a week, paid my bills, and had enough money left over for a couple of twelve packs at the end of the week.

"Open up, fucker. It's your best friend you haven't seen or talked to in over a week!" Meg yelled as she pounded on the front door.

I opened the door, and Meg stood on the other side, her hand raised to pound on the door again. "How the hell did you know I was here?"

"I happened to be driving by and saw your truck. Let me in," she demanded as she pushed past me.

"I'm about to leave, Meg. I still have to run to Marley's and pick up some stuff she wanted." I slammed the door shut and crossed my arms over my chest.

"You can spare five minutes for me, ass." Meg plopped down on the couch and kicked her feet up on the coffee table.

"You could have called me, you know. The phone does work both ways."

"I know that, do you?"

"What do you want, Meg? I know I haven't been to work in a week, and you miss me, but coming over and harassing me seems a bit over the top."

"Oh well, you know me. Over the top is my specialty."

"We all know that well,"

"All right, since I'm on a time limit, I'll just cut straight to the point. How are you and Marley? Scared shitless?"

And right there was the freaky thing about Meg. She knew me. Too well sometimes. "I'm, well, you know, getting used to it."

"You're scared shitless, Troy. Admit it."

I wasn't scared per say, it was more like I didn't know what the hell to do. Oh hell, who was I kidding? I was ready to rip a page out of Marley's book and get the hell out of dodge. "I have no idea what the hell I am doing, Meg. Things are fucking perfect right now. How the hell is that possible? We don't even know each other."

"I think you know each other more than you think."

"This shit doesn't happen. You don't have such strong feelings barely two weeks into knowing someone."

"Now you know how I felt with Lo. It scared the ever living shit out of me that a man like Lo could look at me the way he did so soon. That shit happens in the books I read, not my life. But it did happen to me Troy, and I think it's happening even faster to you, too."

"So what the hell do I do? I can't give her much. This is all I have," I said as I stretched my arms wide.

Meg looked around and shook her head. "This," she twirled her finger over her head, "is not what Marley wants."

"Then what the fuck does she want with me?"

Meg stood up and pulled her truck keys out of her pocket. "She wants the man who is my best friend. The man who helped Cyn when she was hurt. The man who is doing everything in his power to keep her safe. I can guaran-damn-tee that is what she wants. Everything else is irrelevant."

"What if you're wrong? What if she gets sick of the man I am? I don't have a fancy job and a vault full of money."

"Then you let her go and find the girl who is looking for exactly what you are. But, I don't think you'll have to worry about that. I'm going to tell you the same thing Ethel tells me, 'Let that boy in.' Meg's eyes bugged out, and she waved her hand. "Well, substitute girl for boy. Whatever, you get the point."

"It was going pretty good until you called me a girl."

Meg ran her fingers through her hair and brushed it to the side. "Yeah, not everyone can be Ethel."

"You'll have to work on your closing more," I laughed.

"Ugh, I'm out. All this sappy shit is making me miss Lo. I gotta find him and hug the shit out of him." Meg walked up to me, just stared at me.

"You're going to hug me, aren't you?"

Meg got a big loopy smile on her face and wrapped her arms around me. "You're gonna be fine, Troy," she whispered in my ear.

She walked out the door. Her truck fired up, and she was gone before I could say a word.

I grabbed my bag, locked the door behind me and made my way over to my truck.

I made it over to Marley's in less than ten minutes and grabbed the key from under the rock she had texted me about. As I was walking in the door, my phone went off for a text message, and I pulled it out of my pocket as I shut the door behind me.

You have seventeen minutes left before I come looking for you. I guess I couldn't say she didn't care about me.

Just got to your house. Be back to you soon. It was a twenty-minute drive back to the apartment so I would need to hurry the hell up and go about twenty over the speed limit to make it back to her.

I'm counting the seconds.

I'll always come back to you, Sunshine. Damn, I was turning into a sap, but it felt so right. I needed to let Marley know I was missing her as much as she was missing me.

I'll always be waiting.

I shoved my phone back in my pocket before I texted any more sappy shit.

As I was making my way up the stairs, I thought I heard footsteps in the kitchen. I stopped to listen but didn't hear anything. I shook my head, thinking I was losing it and made my way up the rest of the stairs.

I flipped the light on in Marley's room and knew instantly I wasn't hearing things.

"You're not who we were expecting, but we'll make this work." There was a man sitting on the edge of Marley's bed, his hands clasped in front of him. He was wearing a dark blue pinstriped suit and looked like he had stepped off the cover of some fancy magazine. "Grab him."

I turned around and ran into a wall of a man who spun me back around and twisted my arms behind my back.

"Where is Marley?" The man demanded.

"I don't know."

"You know what I hate, Troy?" Oh shit. My idea of playing stupid might not work. This either had to be the Banachi's or Mark's family. "I hate a liar."

"I don't know where she is."

"Then what are you doing in her house right now? You know, I don't care. I don't have time for this." Suit stood up, straitening his jacket.

He walked past me, whispered something to the guy who was holding me and walked out of the room.

That was the last thing I remember before the lights went out and everything went black.

--*-*-*-*-*-*-*

Chapter 25

Marley

"He should be here by now, Gravel!" I yelled as I ate dinner at the kitchen island. It had been over an hour since Troy had texted me. I had tried calling him ten times, and he didn't answer. I knew something was wrong.

"You two have been together for the past week. He's probably just taking a breather. Grab your fork and eat. I'm sure he'll be here any minute," he said as he shoveled more food into his mouth.

I couldn't believe this. Something could have happened to Troy, and Gravel was acting like nothing was going on.

"Just calm down and eat, hun. If Troy isn't back soon, Gravel will start looking and making some phone calls. I'm sure he's ok." Ethel handed me a plate and gently pushed me to sit next to Gravel.

I took a deep breath and looked down at my plate. Ethel and Gravel were right. I'm sure Troy got held up doing something else. I put a small helping of food on my plate and sat down.

"Just breathe, darlin'," Gravel said quietly as he wiped his hands on a napkin.

"I'm sorry. I've already lost one man I cared about."

Ethel stood on the other side of the island, her plate full and she smiled at me. "I know exactly how you feel, hun. When I lost Henry, I didn't think I would ever be able to love another man and then your father came along and showed me love I never thought I would have again."

"I don't love Troy, I just don't want anything to happen to him." I ducked my head, not wanting Ethel to see that I might love Troy. They would think I was crazy if they thought I was in love with a man that I barely knew. Hell, I thought I was crazy for feeling the way I did.

Gravel grunted and shook his head. "I might not be the biggest fan of that cowboy you've fallen in love with darlin', but I can tell you one thing."

"Gravel, be nice," Ethel warned.

"Hush, woman," Gravel said as he winked at Ethel. She shook her head and waited to hear what he had to say. "That boy loves you. And for some damn reason, you love that boy." Gravel shook his head. Apparently talking about Troy made him grunt. "I doubt anything has happened to him, but if it makes you feel better, I'll give King a call and talk to him." Gravel pushed his plate back and stood up.

"You can wait until you're done eating, Gravel." I insisted.

"I'll be back in a few seconds after I figure what happened to Cowboy. Probably saw a cow on the side of the road he had to go look at," Gravel grumbled as he walked out the door.

Ethel and I looked at each other. What the hell did Gravel just say? "Did he just say Troy probably stopped to look at a cow?"

Ethel threw her head back and laughed. "You caught that too. I swear that man is going crazy. He says something nice and then he has to mention cows and loses all credibility."

I shoveled a forkful of meatloaf into my mouth and moaned. Holy crap. Ethel was right about her meatloaf. Is was phenomenal. "Oh my god. That is more than meatloaf," I said around a mouthful.

Ethel beamed at me and laughed. "Told you so. No one can resist my meatloaf. Gravel said the same thing you did before I made it for him. Now he asks for it once a week."

"Remember to invite me over whenever you make it." I shoveled in a huge bite into my mouth and savored it.

Just as I was about to swallow, Gravel came storming back into the house, and I knew something was wrong the second I saw him. The mouthful of food I had in my mouth turned sour, and I couldn't swallow. I grabbed the nearest napkin and spit into it. "What's wrong?" I asked, wiping my mouth.

"We all need to head to the clubhouse. Now," Gravel ordered.

"Why, what's wrong? Where's Troy?" I could feel the panic crawl up my stomach and begin to choke me. Something had happened to Troy.

"King doesn't have all the details yet, and I don't want to worry you any more than necessary."

"Tell me what you know, Gravel!" I yelled. I needed to know what the hell was going on.

"All he knows right now is Mark's family has Troy."

"What do you mean they have Troy? What the hell do you want with Troy? He had nothing to do with them!"

"Marley, you need to calm down, and we need to get to the clubhouse. King said he'll explain more then." Gravel helped Ethel put everything into the fridge, and I just sat there, motionless.

This was exactly what I was afraid of happening. This was why I wanted to leave in the first place. Someone I cared about was hurt because of me. Troy had been kidnapped, and it was all my fault. I felt the tears start to fall, but I didn't stop them.

"Come on, hun. Grab your shoes and we'll get going." Ethel wrapped her arms around me and helped me up. I numbly walked over to the door and slid on my shoes. Ethel handed me Troy's sweatshirt, and I held it up to my nose and inhaled his scent I had grown so used to. I slipped it over my head and wrapped my arms around my middle.

Ethel led me over to her car, and we all climbed in, neither of us talking. There wasn't much to say. Troy was in trouble, and it was all my fault.

--*-*-*-*-*-*-*-*

TROY

My body slammed against something hard, and my eyes cracked open. I had no idea where I was. It was pitch black, and all I could tell was that I was in the trunk of a car that was speeding down the road.

My whole head felt like it was going to explode and I had the metallic taste of blood in my mouth. My bottom lip felt swollen like it had been busted open.

The car careened around a corner, and my head slammed into the side of the trunk. The tires squealed as we made another sharp turn, then I rolled forward as they slammed on the brakes. The car halted to a stop, and I felt it shift into park. Where ever the hell we were going, we were there.

I didn't know how long we had been driving and how long I had been knocked out. All I remember was my head being smashed in and everything going dark.

"Get him and bring him in. I need to make a phone call, and then we'll deal with him."

I still had no idea who the guy in the suit was. King was supposed to be meeting with the Banachi's today. Maybe things hadn't gone the way we had hoped. I had to come up with a plan. How the hell was I going to get out of this?

I heard the key turn in the lock, and I realized I had seconds to figure out what the hell I was going to do. The trunk lip started to rise up, and I did the only thing I could think of.

When the lid was half way up, I kicked up, knocking the trunk lid out of the goon's hand. I jumped out of the trunk as the lid knocked the guy back. I didn't take one thing into account, though. I had kicked the lid so hard it sprang open and slammed back down, slamming into my already battered head.

Son of a bitch. I heard the asshole laughing on the other side at me, and I growled. There had to be a way to get out of this. I just had to bide my time and wait for the right moment.

--*-*-*-*-*-*-*

Chapter 26

Marley

"What the hell is going on? Why would they take Troy? I thought you were going to fix this?" I ranted as I walked in the door of the clubhouse, talking to King.

"As far I knew it was taken care of. Sit down, Marley," King ordered, his voice stern.

"I don't want to sit, I want to go find Troy!" Normally King intimidated me, but right now I didn't give a flying fuck about anything but finding Troy. I had left his apartment scared and afraid, but now I was pissed and wanted answers.

"Marley, sit your ass down and hear what King has to say," Gravel gruffed, grabbing my arm and pulling me over to one of the card tables.

I plopped down in the chair and glared at Gravel. "I'm sitting, now tell me what the hell is going on."

King shook his head and ran his fingers through his hair, sitting next to me. "It's not the Banachi's. I met with them hours ago and everything on their end had been cleared up. It has to be Mark's family doing this. I met with Leo, the head of the Banachi's, and he said he would let Mark's family know they were backing off from you. I'm assuming they didn't take the news well."

"So what the hell are we going to do? We can't just sit here and do nothing. I know he's not part of the Devil's Knights, but we have to help him. YOU have to help him, King!" I was beyond frantic.

"How the ever living fuck did Troy get kidnapped?" Meg shouted as she walked in the door. "I just saw him when he was at his house earlier." Meg stopped in front of King, her hands resting on her hips, waiting for an answer.

"I told Mickey not to tell you anything, just to bring you here."

"Yeah well, I have a special effect on Mick, we've come to an understanding." Meg glanced behind her and winked at Mickey as he walked in the door.

"What the hell! What happened to I swear I won't say a word?" King asked, standing up and walking past Meg.

"Have you met your ol' lady? You can't say no to her. I had no choice!" Mickey raised his hands up in surrender.

"Unbelievable," King scrubbed his hand down his face and shook his head. "You," King turned around, pointing at Meg, "are not to talk to any of the guys anymore. You're making them all your best friends. Stop it."

"Are you serious? I can't help it if I'm likable. You should try being nice sometimes and they'll start listening to you!" Meg shouted, charging at King.

"I'm not here to be liked, Meg," he growled low.

"Enough!" Gravel yelled. "Can we figure out what the hell happened to Troy and then you two can go work out what the hell has crawled up your asses."

"This is not over," King said, staring Meg down.

"Not by a longshot, caveman," Meg whispered vehemently. They stared each other down, neither one blinking.

No one said a word, not knowing what the hell to do. I think we were all witnessing the first fight between Meg and King. Normally I'd be all for grabbing the popcorn and watching the fireworks between the two, but right now we needed to figure out what happened to Troy.

"Um, can we get back to Troy, and ya'll rip each other's clothes off later?" I asked.

"Hmm, I'm gonna rip something off other than his clothes," Meg whispered, walking away from King and sat down next to me.

King growled low and threatening. He ran his fingers through his hair, and I could tell he was trying to calm down.

"I put a call into Leo. He said he'll try to get in touch with Mark's family. Right now we just wait. Cyn and Rigid should be here any minute. I also have Gambler bringing Gwen in. I tried to think of anyone who is connected to you. They were obviously going after the people you care about." King's phone rang, and he walked down the hall, Gravel following him.

"Are you ok, hun?" Meg asked, placing her hand on mine and squeezed.

"Yeah, I was scared before, but now I'm pissed off. I don't know why they took Troy."

"King is probably right. They couldn't get you, so they are going after the people you care about. He'll get this all cleared up." She smiled at me and patted my hand.

"Would you take your hand off of me? I can walk through a door without tripping or getting kidnapped," Gwen said through gritted teeth as she walked through the door, wrenching her arm out of Gambler's grasp.

"Look here, sugar, I'm just doing what King told me to do. If you don't like it, you can take it up with him," Gambler shot back.

"Here's an idea, why don't you think for yourself instead of doing what The King tells you what to do." Gwen swung her purse at Gambler and socked him in the shoulder.

"Did she just call Lo The King?" Meg whispered.

"I think so," I giggled.

"Good Lord, please don't let Lo hear that, it'll go straight to his head." Meg shook her head and sat back in her chair.

"You're here, my job is done." Gambler held his hands up in surrender and headed down the hall Gravel and King had just gone down.

"What the hell is going on, Marley? I was closing up the shop when that bonehead who has been watching me for the past week came up to me and basically kidnapped me and brought me here. He wouldn't tell me what the hell was going on." Gwen walked over to us, tossing her purse on the table and plopped down in the chair across from me.

"Mark's family kidnapped Troy," Meg said, grabbing Gwen's purse, looking at it. "Where did you get this?"

"Kohl's, on sale," Gwen winked at Meg.

"We have got to go shopping together," Meg gushed.

"I'm down whenever you are, girl."

"Hello, Troy getting kidnapped?" I said, waving my hands in their faces.

"Sorry," Meg said, petting Gwen's purse as she set it back down.

"So what's going on? Troy getting kidnapped sucked, but why am I here?" Gwen opened her purse, grabbing out gum and popped a piece in her mouth. Gwen always had gum in her mouth. The only time I had ever seen her without it was when she was eating. She offered a piece to Meg and me.

"Right now we don't know much. The reason you are here is because King thinks they might be going after everyone Marley cares about. Cyn is on the way right now. Oh, shit, where's Ethel?" Meg grabbed her phone out of her purse and was calling Ethel before I could speak.

I heard Ethel's phone ringing from the kitchen and laughed. "Hello?" I heard her say.

"Where the hell are you, Ethel? You need to get to the clubhouse right now!" Meg ordered.

"I'm in the kitchen, Meg." Again, I could hear Ethel talking from the kitchen, but apparently, Meg couldn't.

"Well, get out of the kitchen and get here." Meg ended the call and shoved her phone in her pocket. "I can't believe Gravel didn't bring Ethel. Just leaves her in the kitchen." Meg shook her head and rolled her eyes.

"Who wants a turkey sandwich?" Ethel asked as she breezed out of the kitchen, a huge smile on her face.

"What the hell are you doing here? You told me you were in the kitchen?" Meg asked, stunned.

"I was in the kitchen," Ethel laughed, setting the plate on the table and taking the last chair.

"Hmm, next time specify which kitchen. Now I feel like a dope. I don't know why I didn't think you were here. I couldn't believe that Gravel would have left you home." Meg grabbed a sandwich, ripping off a huge chunk.

"I know, but I thought I'd mess with you, plus you didn't really give me time to talk." Ethel winked.

Meg blushed and shoved the rest of the sandwich in her mouth.

"I'm Gwen." Gwen held her hand out, greeting Ethel.

"Ethel, hun. I'm King's mom and Gravel's fiancée."

"Who's King?" Gwen asked, grabbing a sandwich.

"King is mine, although at the moment claiming him is iffy," Meg stood up and headed for the kitchen.

"Trouble in paradise?" Gwen whispered.

"Ha, no. More like Meg is crazy and King just tries to reel her in sometimes." Ethel whispered.

"I heard that!" Meg yelled. "You're supposed to be on my side, Ethel, even though he's your son." Meg walked back over to the table, handing us each a bottle of water.

"I'm on your side, hun," Ethel winked.

"No taking sides," Lo gruffed as he walked back into the common room. "We're on the same team, babe."

Meg rolled her eyes, but a blush rose on her cheeks. "Stop being nice, I'm supposed to be pissed at you."

"Try another day, babe." Lo literally picked Meg up off her chair and sat down with her in his lap.

"Manhandling me now?" Meg whispered, cuddling into his embrace.

"He's The King?" Gwen asked, her jaw dropped as she looked King up and down. Lo really was something to look at. With his signature ripped jeans and tight tees, he even made me do a double-take the first time I met him.

"Just King. You must be Gwen," Lo held his hand out to Gwen, and she just stared at it.

She looked at me, her eyes bugged out. "I feel like he's royalty. Do I kiss his hand and curtsey?"

Meg threw her head back laughing, and King wrapped both of his arms around her so she didn't fall out of his lap. "You can touch him," she wheezed, grabbing on to King.

"Babe, you're crazy," King laughed, brushing back the hair from her face.

"Now that the introductions are over, do you think maybe we could focus on finding Troy?" I was beyond frantic, and here we were, sitting around shooting the shit.

"There isn't much we can do right now, Marley. We're waiting to hear back from Leo," Gravel said, walking out of the kitchen, a beer dangling from his fingertips.

"Are you shitting me?" I slammed my fists down on the table. All eyes turned to me, shocked. "We're going to put Troy's life in the hands of a man who not even four hours ago was trying to kill me? Are you all insane?"

"Calm down, hun. We're doing everything we can," Ethel said, patting my hand.

I snatched my hand away, not wanting to be pacified. "We should be out there looking for him. We should call the god damn police is what we should do." I pulled my phone from my pocket and fanatically tried calling 911.

Just as I had the dial pad pulled up, King snatched my phone out of my hand and handed it to Meg. She looked at me with sympathy but shoved it in her pocket.

"You call the police, Marley, we are going to have an even bigger problem on our hands. Just let us figure it out. I promise nothing will happen to Troy." King leveled his gaze at me, waiting.

Son of a bitch, he was right. I'm sure the Banachi's didn't deal with the police well. From what I have heard, they worked above the police.

So what the hell was I supposed to do then? I couldn't sit around twiddling my thumbs waiting for something to happen. "Fine, no police. Can we at least go and look for him?"

"Marley, where the hell are we even going to begin looking for him? Sit tight, darlin' and everything will work out." Gravel stood behind me and rest his hands on my shoulder.

"Oh, I have an idea!" Meg jumped up from King's lap and ran into the kitchen.

"Ten bucks she's going for the bottle of Southern," Gambler said, holding his hand out to Crowbar.

"I ain't taking that bet. King told all of us how she handles stress. I'm out on that bet, man." Crowbar held his hands up in surrender and plopped down on the sofa in front of a big screen TV.

"I'll take that bet," Slider pulled a ten dollar bill out of his pocket and held it up. Gambler pulled one from his wallet and tossed it onto the table.

"Any other takers?" Gambler looked around.

King pulled a twenty out of his wallet and threw it on the table. "I'll double that bet."

"You for or against the Southern?"

"Hmm, I'm going to go against my gut and say she's grabbing something else." King leaned back in his chair, kicking his feet back and threw his hands over his head.

"You sure about that?" Gambler asked.

"Yeah, I got faith in Meg."

We waited, hearing nothing but silence from the kitchen. "What do you think she's doing?" Gwen whispered.

"Lord only knows with Meg. You stick around long enough you'll see for yourself." Crowbar said and winked at Gwen. Gambler elbowed Crowbar, and I swear I thought I heard him growl.

Crowbar looked at him like he was crazy and rubbed his arm. "What the fuck, brother?"

Gambler just shook his head, not saying anything.

"Who wants to play Go Fish?" Meg asked, holding up a deck of cards.

"Shit," Gambler said, throwing his hands up in the air. "You were supposed to be getting a bottle of Southern," he complained.

"Why the hell would I go to the kitchen to get a bottle of Southern? I would have walked over to your fully stocked bar." Meg gestured to the bar that spanned the whole wall of the clubhouse.

"Son of a bitch!" Gambler shouted, pissed off.

"You shouldn't bet against my woman, brother," King taunted as he collected the money off the table and took the other ten Gambler was holding out. He gave half to Crowbar and pocketed the rest.

"How long do we have to wait until we hear from the Banachi's?" I was losing it. As much as everyone was trying to distract me, it wasn't enough.

"Leo said he would call back in an hour regardless of what he found out. I told him the sooner, the better, darlin'," King reassured me.

Meg sat down on his lap and opened the cards. "I can't shuffle unless ya'll feel like playing fifty-two card pickup."

"Give 'em here," Gambler grumbled. "They don't call me Gambler for nothing."

So here I sat, playing cards while Troy was off somewhere possibly being tortured and beaten all because he was someone I knew.

I'd like my normal life back anytime now.

--*-*-*-*-*-*-*-*

Chapter 27

TROY

"Leo is on the way over, boss, and he did not sound happy."

"He'll see my side of things when he gets here. No one is going to take all that money away from me. Especially that little rat Mark got tangled up with." I had finally figured out who the hell had kidnapped me. It was Mark's family. I assumed King's meeting with the Banachi's did not go as planned.

Right now I was in a hotel room outside of town, sitting on the bed with my arms tied behind my back; the rope tied to the bed frame. I still had no idea why they thought kidnapping me would help them. I would let them kill me before I told them where Marley was.

"Alright, I'll wait out front for them." The guy who had clocked me over the head walked out the door, leaving it ajar.

"Bet you didn't know what you were getting into when you decided to get your dick wet in that whore," Pinstriped suit sneered at me while grabbing a briefcase from the floor and setting it on the desk.

"You might want to rethink the next thing that comes out of your mouth if it has anything to do with Marley." I tugged on the rope on my wrists, trying to loosen it.

"Dumb bitch has got you all tied up in knots, too. Must have a magical pussy that one." He opened his briefcase and pulled out a bottle of whiskey and two shot glasses. If this prick hadn't kidnapped me and tied me up, I would have given him credit for having a full bottle of booze in his briefcase instead of paperwork.

"She had my son tripping over himself to get to her, too. Fucking foolish." He sloshed two fingers worth of whiskey in each glass and put the bottle back in his briefcase.

"Your son had good taste," I muttered.

"That's where you are wrong. My son had horrible taste. He could have had the pick of the litter in high school and who does he bring home? Some whore from the wrong side of the tracks. The more we asked him to find someone else, the more he dug his feet in and wouldn't leave her. I never should have given him a quarter of my business." He shook his head and tossed back one of the shots.

"She doesn't want the money, asswipe."

"That's where you're wrong. Everyone wants money, even your whore, Marley. It's just an act, I know it." He grabbed the other shot and drank it down. He wiped his mouth with the back of his hand and slammed the glass on the table.

"Look, Kevin, Marley doesn't want shit from your family. She didn't want it when she was with Mark and she sure as shit doesn't want it now," I sneered. I had managed to grab the loose end of the rope and was slowly working it back through the knot.

"Wrong. She wants it. She had Mark pay for her schooling, and he bought her cars and expensive jewelry all the time. I saw the receipts. The web of lies she is spinning wound you right up. She's a money hungry whore."

Marley had mentioned the jewelry to me, and she said she would accept it, but never wear it. I had spent a lot of time with Marley the past few weeks, and she didn't seem materialistic at all. I had to bargain with her to let me buy the black dress at the mall for her, and it didn't even cost that much money. Kevin here was a fucking idiot. Just because he was a money hungry asshole, he thought everyone else was too. "Believe what you want, man, but I know the truth."

He grabbed the glass and threw it across the room, and it shattered against the wall. "No, you look here, *man,* I want my fucking money, and you're god damn whore has got it tied up in so much legal tape, I don't even know if I'll see it before I die!"

"So kidnapping me is going to somehow help you get your money? Newsflash, asswipe, kidnapping and attempted murder don't really look good." I had to keep Kevin talking until I figured out a plan. From what Kevin's goon had said, the Banachi's would be here soon. I didn't know if that was a good thing or not.

"Kidnapping you wasn't part of the plan, but I have to play the cards I was dealt. Leo owes me a favor since he didn't kill Marley. If his plan involves you dying, I'm fine with that." Kevin's lips stretched into a manic smile. Kevin said he would play the cards he was dealt, but I don't think he was playing with a full deck.

"You're fucking crazy. You don't even have a plan." I had managed to get the rope loosened, and I slowly slipped my right hand out. I didn't want to make any sudden movements to alarm Kevin.

"You don't need a plan when you have the Banachi's behind you. My grandfather always told me that. I never had to call in a favor to them before, but I'm glad I did. Leo will have all of this cleared up in no time." Kevin grabbed his suitcase and tossed it on the other bed. It bounced and fell off the side. "Son of a bitch," Kevin cursed as he turned his back to me and bent over to grab it.

Now was the only chance I would have. I jumped up, tackled Kevin and wrapped my arm around his neck. His arms flailed trying to get a grip on me, but he couldn't. I pulled him up, my arm still crushing his neck and we stumbled over to the door. I flicked the lock and swung the deadlock shut.

"Boss, you ok?" I heard the goon holler through the door. The handle jingled as he tried to open it. "Mr. Parks, are you ok?" His voice rose, concerned.

"Mr. Parks is indisposed at the moment," I yelled. Kevin was still struggling against my hold, but I could tell he was having trouble breathing. That one year of wrestling in high school was finally paying off.

I shoved Kevin onto the bed, face down and grabbed the rope they had used to tie me up. I quickly bound his hands behind his back and tied the rope to his feet. Even if he managed to get up, he would trip instantly. The pounding on the door intensified and I knew it was only a matter of minutes before the door was kicked in.

"Marco is going to kill you once he gets the door open," Kevin laughed hysterically.

"He's gonna have to get me first," I mumbled. I loosened my hold on him and backed away slowly. He struggled, trying to get his arms loose but he couldn't.

"You won't get away with this," he screamed.

"I think I just might, Kevy," I smirked. "Hey, Marco!" I called over the pounding and kicking he was doing to the door.

"What," he yelled.

"You kick through that door, I'll kill Kevin the second I see your ugly face." I walked to the bathroom, looking for a window, but there wasn't one. Son of a bitch. I had to get the fuck out of here, but it appeared the only way out was through Marco.

The banging on the door stopped, and I heard mumbled talking outside the door.

Fuck. The Banachi's must be here.

"Mr. Oliver, I'd like to have a word with Mr. Parks." I heard a deep voice call from the other side of the door.

"You are so fucking dead," Kevin laughed. Fucking asswipe.

I didn't have any other choice. Right now, Leo Banachi was my best bet for getting out of here. I unlocked the deadbolt and handle and twisted it to the left. I swung the door open, ready to attack if I had to.

"No need to be alarmed, Mr. Oliver. You are who I'm here for, but it's not for what you think." Leo Banachi walked through the door with Marco following behind. Marco grabbed me by the throat and slammed me against the wall.

I gasped for breath and managed to slug Marco in the gut, knocking the wind out of him. He let go of my neck and doubled over, trying to catch his breath. I landed another punch to the side of his head, and he fell over, grasping his head.

"That's enough Mr. Oliver. I'm sure Marco won't be making any other stupid moves like that." Leo leaned down, his eyes connecting with Marco's. "Will you, Marco?" he asked.

Marco shook his head and stayed on the floor. Leo Banachi was a man who could make even the toughest men cower.

Leo walked over to Kevin and stood over him. "I thought we had discussed things, Kevin, and you had agreed to find another way to get your money that didn't involve Marley." Leo's tone was pure disapproving.

"There is no other way to get my money. Even you said that when we had first discussed killing her. It's the only way," Kevin insisted.

"Well, my mind has been changed. I told you I had a meeting with King from the Devil's Knights, and we were going to have to go about things a different way."

"If we go through the courts, I'm not going to see that money until I die!"

Leo shook his head and pulled his phone out of his pocket. He pressed a couple of buttons and held it to his ear. "I'm going to need you in here. Things are unfortunately not going how I want them to." Leo pressed the end button and slid the phone back in his pocket. "Is he tied up tightly?"

"Ugh, it should hold him," I muttered.

"Good. Oscar will be in to take care of Mr. Parks and Marco."

"He's not going to be able to hurt Marley, is he?" I asked. I wasn't exactly sure on what was going on, but from what I gathered, Kevin had gone off the rails, and Leo Banachi was here to clean up.

"I have a feeling Kevin Marks will be going on vacation and coming back with a whole new attitude." Leo gestured to the door for us to leave. I glanced back at Kevin, feeling bad for the guy for having to encounter Leo's wrath that was coming to him.

We walked out of the hotel room as another man in a pinstripe suit walked by us. He nodded his head at Leo and quietly clicked the door shut behind him. I heard the locks slide into place and knew Kevin's attitude adjustment was about to begin.

"You need a ride home?" I finally took a good look at Leo and saw he wasn't much older than I was. He had your typical business man look to him, but you could also see there was a deadly edge to him.

"Uh, you don't have to go out of your way. I dropped my phone somewhere, so if I could borrow your phone, I'm sure I can get King or someone to pick me up."

"I'll take you to King. I have a business proposition I want to run by him before I head back home anyway. I can kill two birds with one stone this way." Leo pulled a set of keys out of his wrinkle-free dress pants and headed to a black, sleek Mercedes.

I stood, there not following. What the hell was going on? Ten minutes ago I was five seconds away from getting my head smashed in, and now Leo Banachi was offering me a ride. I glanced up at the sky, seeing the moon high in the sky and wondered what the hell time it was. Being knocked out and bound to a bed makes you lose track of time.

It was hard to believe earlier today I had told Marley I would be back to her in an hour. I bet she was freaking out, blaming herself for everything. I couldn't blame her for what happened, though. She didn't know Mark's family was going to go completely insane and try to kill her and me.

"You taking the ride with me, or you gonna stare at the sky all night?" Leo called. I glanced at him, the driver's side door open, one leg in the car, waiting for me.

I glanced back at the hotel room, hearing the sickening thud of Oscar's fists connecting with Kevin. Things could finally go back to normal. Marley didn't need to look over her shoulder all the time now, wondering if someone was after her and I didn't need to be there to protect her.

With everything cleared up, would Marley still want me there?

"You think we could swing by my house?" I asked as I opened the passenger door and looked at Leo.

"I got nothing but time on my hands right now." Leo slid into the car, slamming his door shut behind him.

I guess it was time to find out if Marley and I were just a one-night stand or something more.

--*-*-*-*-*-*-*-*

Chapter 28

Marley

"Call him, now! I don't care if he's Leo fucking Banachi! It's been over an hour since he said he would call." I was past frantic and scared and had entered terrified and hysterical.

I had only managed to play a half a game of Go Fish before I tossed my cards down and began pacing the room. Ethel had tried dragging me into the kitchen to make more food, but I wasn't having any of that.

"Oh my god, if you pace that floor one more time, I'm tackling and sitting on you until we find Troy," Meg called from behind the bar. She had lasted forty-five minutes before she snuck behind the bar and grabbed the bottle of Southern.

"I can't help it! We're just sitting here not doing anything! Is this what ya'll did when tweedle dee and tweedle dumb took me?"

"Ha! No. That could have also been because we didn't know you were kidnapped until they basically turned you free," Cyn said from her perch from up on the bar.

Cyn and Rigid had shown up just after the first card game and had jumped in on trying to distract me. King had disappeared ten minutes ago and hadn't come back yet. I had tried following him down the hallway, but Gravel had grabbed me before I was even two steps down the hall. "Calm down, Marley. King has things under control," Gravel had said.

I had ripped my arm out of his grasp and huffed back to the common room and continued my pacing.

"That's it, I'm sitting on you," Meg said, slamming the bottle down on the bar. She rounded the long bar, mischief playing in her eyes and darted at me. I managed to side step her and ducked to the left.

"You're crazy!" I shouted as I ran around the tables, glancing behind me to see Meg gaining on me.

"Just sit your ass down!"

"I thought we were friends!" Everyone was laughing and shouting at Meg to get me. I repeat, Meg was crazy.

"We are friends. We have to be friends, you're in love with my best friend."

"What?" I yelled, looking back Meg. How the hell did she know I was in love with Troy? I hadn't even admitted fully to myself yet.

"You love him. If you didn't, you wouldn't be pacing around like a mad woman."

"I barely know him."

"Like that freaking matters. If I look back at Lo and me, I loved him after a week. Not that I'll ever tell him that."

I was close to the front door and figured my only escape was to dart out the door. Just as I had the handle in my hand, the door burst open and knocked me on my ass.

"Oh shit," Meg cursed. "That had to hurt." I heard her mumble.

I looked up to the see who had opened the door and my jaw dropped. Troy was standing over me, a confused look on his face.

"What the hell were you doing standing behind the door?" He asked, crouching down in front of me.

"What are you doing here?" Yup, this whole time I had been freaking out that Troy was kidnapped, and now he was here, and I wanted to know why.

"Um, I thought you might be worried about me."

"Worried about you? Fuck, she was driving us insane. Thank god you're back," Meg huffed.

"Glad to see you're so concerned, Meg."

"Hey, I was worried, but it's not like you're some defenseless little girl. You're Troy. I knew you'd find a way to get out." Meg crossed her arms over her chest and walked over to King, who was talking to a guy I had never seen before.

"You want help up, Sunshine?" Troy stood up and held his hand out to me.

"Ow, my ass is going to hurt for days," I moaned as he pulled me up. I rubbed my butt and winced.

"Your ass is getting more attention than me right now," Troy laughed.

"Oh my God, Troy, I'm so glad you're ok," Ethel gushed, walking up to Troy and wrapped him up in a hug.

"I'm good, Ethel. Just a bit sore." He smiled and winked at me over Ethel's shoulder.

"Just because Marley got kidnapped before didn't mean you had to, too," Ethel scolded, stepping back.

"I couldn't let her have all the fun," Troy smirked.

"Are you hungry? You missed dinner. It's almost nine o'clock."

"I'll eat in a little bit," he said, glancing at me.

"I'll throw something together. Meg has been keeping the kitchen here stocked lately." Ethel wandered to

223

the kitchen, quietly mumbling under her breath about lunch meat.

"My turn!" Cyn yelled, running over to Troy. She launched herself at him, and he took a step back as he caught her so they both didn't fall.

"Good Lord, Cyn," Troy grunted.

"I'm glad you're ok, homie."

"I have no idea why you call me homie," Troy laughed, shaking his head.

"Cause you're my homie," Cyn said like that explained everything.

"King and I knew you'd have things under control." Rigid walked over and pulled Cyn from Troy. He wrapped his arms around her from behind and rested his chin on the top of her head.

"You're squishing me." Cyn elbowed Rigid in the gut, trying to get away from him and almost got away. He swung her up in his arms and tossed her on the couch in front of the TV. Rigid jumped on top of her, and all we could hear was squealing and laughing.

"You think I could get a hug now, Sunshine?"

I tore my eyes away from the spectacle going on on the couch and saw Troy had never taken his eyes off me.

I was two steps away from Troy when King called his name. "Troy!"

Son of a bitch. "I'll be right back, baby girl," Troy murmured. He trailed his fingers down my arm as he walked past me, but that was all I got.

Troy walked over to King and the man I had never seen before and headed down the hallway. Rigid and all the other members followed behind leaving all the women behind.

"Well, I'm going to head home as soon as I hot wire a car," Gwen said picking up her purse and hitching it over her shoulder.

"Ha, funny," Meg laughed.

"Oh, it's not funny, sweetheart. I know how to do a lot more than hot wire a car."

Meg and Cyn's jaws dropped, and Ethel shook her head. I knew Gwen had a hard life growing up, so I had no doubt that she wasn't joking.

"Well, you can give me a ride home after you find a car to steal," I laughed.

"Guys, I have my car, I can take ya'll home." Cyn held up her keys, shocked.

"Hell, just take my truck," Meg grabbed her keys out of her pocket and tossed them to Gwen. "Lo and I drove separate. I'll swing by your house tomorrow to get it."

"Are you sure that Troy wants you leaving?" Cyn asked.

"Just tell Troy I'll see him later. I have something at home I need to do." Gwen walked out the door, holding it open for me.

"Wait," Meg called, grabbing my arm and halting me in my tracks. "I can't let you go if you're going to run, Marley. I can't let you hurt Troy like that."

I shook my head and laughed, "The only place I am going is to my house. If Troy is worried, tell him to come find me when he is done here."

"He won't be long. I know he wants to see you."

"Just tell him I'm at home, ok, Meg." She let go of my arm and looked at me like she would never see me again. I made it to the door and turned around. "I'm glad he had a friend like you in his life, Meg. Not everyone gets that." I walked out the door, hearing it click shut behind me.

"You ok, doll?" Gwen asked as I climbed into Meg's truck.

"I'm not really sure. I'm terrified, but I'm not going to run. Troy might not come over tonight. His job of protecting me is done. I was an obligation before, and now I have to be something he chooses."

"I saw the way he looked at you, doll. There's more there than you think." Gwen started the truck, and we headed out the parking lot.

"I hope you're right, Gwen. I want him so much, but I need him to want me as much."

"Don't stress about it. Everything works out. Just look at it this way. Six months ago, you lost your fiancée and didn't know what you were going to do. Now you have a kick ass job with a bitchin' boss, reconnected with your dad, new friends from what I just saw, and one smoking hot guy who I *know* has the hots for you."

"But it could all go away in an instant."

"Marley," Gwen took her eyes off the road and glanced at me. "You of all people know that things can change in an instant. But maybe in that instant, they can change for the better. You're never going to know unless you take the risk and see if the risk is worth the fall."

"OK, you're right. Take me home, I've got a plan," I smiled, finally believing the only way to be happy was to lay all my cards on the table and let the chips fall where they may.

The first thing I was going to do when I got home was unpack all my boxes and prove to Troy that I was here to stay, and nothing was going to make me run.

Not even falling in love with the man I had been waiting my whole life for but never knew existed. Time to stop fighting my feelings for Troy and take what I wanted.

--*-*-*-*-*-*-*-*

Chapter 29

TROY

"Before you called me, King, I had an interesting phone call from a man who went by the name Big A."

Holy shit. Leo, King, and the rest of the Devil's Knights were gathered in the room where they normally held church.

I hadn't wanted to leave Marley, but I knew something had to be up when King had called my name. I was standing by the door, my arms crossed over my chest, waiting to hear what the hell Leo was talking about.

"Why would Big A get in touch with you?" King asked.

"Well, he had somehow found out we were contracted by Mr. Mark and he thought we might be interested in helping him take out a man named, Rigid."

Rigid growled and slammed his fist down on the table. "That fucking cocksucker."

"He informed me all that had been going on between the two of you. I always like to know all the facts before I back the winning horse. Mr. Big A does not appear to be the winning horse to me." Leo rested his elbows on the counter and steepled his hands in front of him.

"So where does that leave us?" King asked.

"Well, Big A continued to go on and say he wouldn't feel bad at all if something were to happen to Mr. Rigid or all the Devil's Knights for that matter."

"Did he tell you anything more, where they were?"

"No, he did ask to have a meeting with me to discuss things further. I told him I would have to think things over and get back to him. He said he would give me two days to decide if I wanted to help him."

"I guess the question to ask is if you are planning on helping him," King said, leaning back in his chair.

"I make very decisive decisions and don't back away from them. Five minutes into my conversation with Big A, I knew what I was going to do. The only thing I fear is that my decision might bring repercussions to the Devil's Knights. Big A is going to try and take each and every one of you out, regardless if I help him or not."

"So what the hell are we going to do? We're basically in the same spot we were before. We know the Assassins are after us, but we don't know where they are," Demon said.

"Well, this is where my proposition comes in. I am more than willing to offer any help you could use in getting rid of your problem with the Assassins if you help me with my own situation my nephew has gotten himself into."

"And what situation would that be?"

"Well, it would be my nephew and sister you would be helping out. My nephew, Antonio, got a little too big for his britches and started stirring things up with a local gang. Small potatoes really, but it would best for his mother and him to leave town for a bit, if not longer."

"So what exactly do you want us to do?"

"I just need a quiet place for them to lay low until I get things under control. Right now they are staying at our estate in Martha's Vineyard, but we rent it out during the fall and winter. Our first renters will be there in three weeks. They would arrive on the first of November and more than likely stay until the first of the year. I will pay for all their lodging and such, but I would ask for you to look after them and make sure nothing happens to them."

"What exactly did your nephew do to get on the wrong side of this gang?" Slider asked.

"I deal in, let's say, undesirable things. I know you've all gone legit, so I know not to bring that business aspect to your door. Antonio got it in his head that he wants to go into the family business and started with small potatoes, mueling drugs. I do not want my life for my nephew. It is a hard life that few can handle."

"So, did he fuck up a drop or something?"

"No, the problem is he was too good at it and started taking business away from the gang who use to do the mueling. I believe that is where your trouble with the Assassins began if I am correct. They thought you were stealing their territory."

"Hard to believe, but yeah, that was what our first meeting with them was about. Then their cousin beat up Rigid's ol' lady, and they didn't like the way we came to a resolution."

"Well, I feel I could help you with your problem with the Assassins and in return, you could look out for my sister and nephew until I get things settled at home."

King looked around the table, gauging everyone's reaction. "I think that could be an even trade. I might know of a place she could rent for a couple of months. I'll talk to Meg and see if she knows of anything."

"All right, we can hammer all the details out later." Leo held his hand out to King, and they shook hands. "I'll be in town until Tuesday. We'll meet again before I leave."

Leo stood up, nodding his head in the direction of all the members and walked out the door.

"Are we all right with what just went down?" King asked, looking around.

"Hell yeah. If it means we get the Assassins off our backs I'm down with babysitting for a couple of months," Demon said. Everyone else nodded their heads and mumbled yes.

"One last thing," King said as everyone started to get up. They all sat down, wondering what else there could be. "Until we get everything wrapped up with the Assassins, we need to keep an eye on everything and everyone. Meg, Cyn, Ethel and Marley need to be with someone at all times. Gambler, you get Gwen and bring her back to the clubhouse."

"What the hell do we need to watch her for?" Gambler groaned.

"I don't want to leave any stone unturned, and I don't want anyone to get hurt just by knowing us. You've been with her the past week, Gambler, so you have her until this is all cleared."

"This is bullshit!" Gambler pushed away from the table. "The fucking chick does everything to annoy the fuck out of me. I won't even tell you what she did to me when I was in the shower this morning."

"What? You finally found a chick that isn't falling at your feet? I think I might like this chick," Gravel laughed.

"Ha ha, yuck it up, assholes," Gambler grumbled as everyone laughed.

"It shouldn't be long. You can handle her for a couple of weeks, Gambler." King didn't leave any more room for argument from Gambler.

"Uh, I see how ya'll don't have a problem keeping an eye on Meg, Cyn, and Ethel because you live with them, but I'm not in the same boat as you guys." All eyes turned to me.

"What the hell are you talking about? You dumping my girl?" Gravel stood and advanced towards me.

"No, but I have no idea what she's thinking. Even if we are together, how the hell do I tell her she needs to move in with me?"

Gravel got right in my face and growled. I swear I could see steam coming out of his ears. "You tell her she's moving in with you, and that's that. You want to be with my daughter, you need to fucking be there when she needs you. Not whenever you want to get your dick wet."

"That's not what I fucking meant." Gravel and I were face to face, ready to rip the other ones head off.

"Then say what the fuck you mean!"

"You're a fucking asshole, you know that?"

"What. The. Hell. Are. You. Doing. With. Marley?"

"I'm pretty sure I should tell Marley that before you, asshole," I bit out.

Gravel and I stared each other down, neither of us backing down.

"Break it up you two," King said, walking in between us. "Do whatever you have to do to keep Marley safe, Troy."

"I'm on it," I growled, turning to the door and stormed out.

Who the fuck did Gravel think he was to demand what I was doing with Marley? He may be her father, but he hadn't been a part of her life for how long, and now he thought he could just roll in and take over where he left off. He may have good intentions, but he was about to get his ass kicked if he didn't back the fuck off.

I had no idea what the hell Marley and I were. Telling her she had to move into my house again until things got taken care of seemed to be pushing the bounds of our relationship I didn't even know the limits of.

"Oh good, you guys are done. Cyn fell asleep on the couch." Meg pointed to Cyn, who was sprawled out on the couch snoring softly.

I looked around the room, noticing Marley and Gwen were nowhere to be seen. "Where the hell did Marley go?" I demanded.

"Um, she and Gwen took my truck and left," Meg mumbled.

"She fucking ran, didn't she?"

Meg looked at me, pity in her eyes. "I honestly don't know. She didn't have the same look in her eyes as the last time. I honestly think she is just trying to figure everything out, Troy."

"She had to run to figure shit out?"

I started pacing the room. I had no idea what the fuck to do. She seemed fine when I left her, but now she was gone. "Do you know where she went?"

"She said she was going home and if you wanted to see her you could go over there. Gwen was going to drop her off at her house, and she said she had something to do."

Yeah, like pack her fucking bags. "Son of a bitch!" I ran my fingers through my hair and stopped in my tracks. She was leaving me again, I fucking knew it.

"I think you need to go talk to her before you assume anything, Troy."

"How the hell do you know, Meg? Do you have the one person you love running every chance they got?"

Meg looked at me shocked, her mouth hanging open. Fuck, I just told Meg I loved Marley. I hadn't even admitted to myself I loved Marley, and now I just blurted it out.

"You love Marley?"

"I don't know, I could," I muttered.

"Holy shit, Troy. That's huge for you. The only thing I've ever heard you say you love is beer and Bandit."

"Yeah, well, I do like beer," I smirked. "Wait, where's Bandit?" Bandit was at the apartment with us, and I hadn't seen him yet.

"King had Remy go pick him up and took him back to my house. I figured he could hang out with Blue tonight, and I'd bring him over tomorrow."

"Thanks," I mumbled.

"Can we get back to the fact that you love Marley?"

I didn't know what to say. Did I love Marley? I sure as hell didn't want her leaving and the idea of having her stay with me pleased me more than it annoyed me.

"Oh my god, you love her! Stop being an ass and go get her!" Meg and I both turned to the couch, surprised to hear Cyn awake.

"Dude, you were snoring like five minutes ago."

"Yeah, well, with you and Troy yapping so loud, you woke me the hell up." Cyn sat up, her head popping up over the back of the couch.

"Why the hell are you sleeping so early anyway?" Meg asked.

"It's what people do when they are tired," Cyn shot back.

"Dude, feisty much?"

"Would you stop saying, dude? You're going to be thirty-seven in three months," Cyn grumbled, laying back down on the couch.

"You're so PMSing aren't you?"

Cyn raised her hand up, flipping the bird. "Sit and spin, Meg."

"You first, babe," Meg laughed.

"You both suck. Go get Marley, Troy and, Meg shut the hell up. I'm freakin' tired." Cyn ordered.

"Gah, you better go. She's grumpier than a hungry bear right now," Meg whispered.

"I don't have a car, remember, I did get kidnapped a couple of hours ago."

"I think we can-" Meg started but was cut off when keys came flying at me, hitting the side of my head.

"Nice shot," Meg laughed.

"Jesus Christ. Have you heard of maybe saying heads up when you throw something," I barked at Cyn, bending down to pick up the keys.

"Have you heard of manning up and taking what you want? You want Marley, fucking take her," Cyn snapped.

"Who the hell pissed you off, beautiful?" Rigid asked, walking into the common room, followed by the rest of the club.

"I think you need to take your woman home," Meg advised Rigid.

"I think you might be right," Rigid said, ducking a pillow that came sailing over the couch. Meg didn't see it in time and got smacked on the side of the head.

"You bitch," Meg spat out. She darted past Rigid and pounced over the back of the couch onto Cyn.

All Rigid and I could see were asses and elbows as Meg and Cyn wrestled each other.

"You really think they're pissed at each other?" Rigid asked, unsure of what the hell was going on.

"Nah," I said, hearing Meg laugh. "You might want to break it up soon before Slider gets out the cooking oil." I nodded towards the kitchen where Slider was searching the cabinets and looked at Rigid and me with a big grin on his face.

"Oh fuck no," Rigid called, moving over to Meg and Cyn. "King, get your woman off mine," he called.

I watched as all the guys made their way over to the couch, trying to see what the hell was going on.

"You hurt her, I'll kill you," I heard growled behind me.

I turned around to see Gravel standing by the bar, his arm around Ethel. Not what I wanted to deal with right now.

"Gravel, would you take the stick out of your ass and just leave Troy alone?" Ethel scolded.

He grunted as she elbowed him in the gut. "Damn, woman."

"I don't ever plan on hurting Marley, Gravel. I know you don't believe that, but I have no problem proving it to you every day you see the smile on Marley's face I put there. Cuss me out and call me names, but just know I will die before I hurt Marley."

Gravel just glared at me, knowing there was nothing he could do or say to keep me away from Marley. "Well, what the hell are you still doing here? You have about fifty years in front of you taking care of my daughter."

I smiled at Ethel, both of us knowing I had finally said the right thing. Gravel was never going to like me, but I, at least, had his respect.

I walked out of the clubhouse unsure of what was going to happen in the next couple of hours but sure of whatever happened, I was doing the one thing I needed to.

I wanted Marley, and I was going to take her.

--*-*-*-*-*-*-*-*-*

Chapter 30

Marley

It had been over an hour since I left the clubhouse and still no Troy. I was beginning to think he wasn't coming.

After Gwen had dropped me at home, I started putting my plan into motion. I needed to know that Troy was there for me and not because he had to be.

I took a shower, making sure to use my expensive body wash I only used when I needed an extra pick me up. I blew out my hair and curled the ends then pulled half of it up letting tendrils cascade around my face.

I went into my closet and knew exactly what I was going to wear. I was going to have to sneak over to Troy's and grab the little black dress, but I knew what shoes I needed. I dug in the bottom of my closet and found my patent leather pumps and tossed them onto the bed.

There were three boxes piled in the corner of my room. I opened them all and quickly put most of it away I had room for and dumped the rest in the back of my closet. I needed to get all of the boxes out of my house. I could find a place for the things I had no idea where they went later.

I ran down to the den, beelining for the five boxes I had there and made quick work putting everything where it belonged. I grabbed all eight empty boxes and ran them down to the curb, groaning as I was halfway there when I realized I was only in a towel. Thankfully it was late enough that no one drove by during my run to the curb in my towel.

I pulled on my dress and heels and almost chickened out ten times before I made it down the stairs. After I had lighted all the candles I had in my living room, I blew them out and then relit them. I was an indecisive mess.

I was now alternating sitting on the couch and pacing the living room waiting for Troy.

After turning on the radio, I put on the song I wanted Troy to hear and let him know I wasn't going anywhere. I had listened to the song nine times and was ready to throw the stereo out the window if I had to listen to it again.

Just as I was about to turn the radio off, there was a knock on the door, and I froze in my tracks. Shit! He was here.

"Marley, open the door," Troy called.

I still didn't move. This is what I had been waiting for, and now I didn't know what the hell to do. He pounded on the door again, snapping me out of my stupor.

I reached for the handle, and I knew it was now or never. Time to stop running and grab the thing I wanted.

Troy stood on the other side of the door looking as terrified as I felt. "You left."

"Um, yeah, I had some things to do." I opened the door wider and stepped out from behind it. Troy's eyes scanned my body, and I heard his intake of breath when he realized what I was wearing.

"Can I come in?" He asked, running his fingers through his hair. I was captivated by him, realizing how often he ran his fingers through his hair and what it did to my sanity. Although it seemed Troy breathing tampered with my sanity.

I stepped to the side, not saying a word and waited for him. He walked past me, his arm brushing against me. I closed the door and leaned against it.

"So why did you have to leave?" he asked, turning around to face me.

"Um, I need to finish unpacking some things."

"You couldn't have waited for me?"

"No, it was something I needed to do on my own."

Troy shook his head and walked into the living room, sitting on the edge of the recliner. "So that's what the pile of boxes on the curb was?"

I pushed away from the door and stood in front of Troy. "Yes."

"It's like pulling teeth talking to you right now, Marley. I don't know what's going on with you right now. You ran from me again."

"I didn't run," I pleaded.

"Then what the hell is going on?"

"I'm terrified. Absolutely scared." I clasped my hands, wringing my hands together.

Troy reached for me, grabbing my hands. "You don't need to be afraid of anything, Marley."

"I know, it's just that I've never done this before. I've never felt the way I do right now, and it seriously makes me want to barf."

Troy threw his head back and laughed. "So I make you feel like you're going to barf?"

My face heated, and I rolled my eyes. "Well, not really."

Troy tugged on my hands and pulled me to him. He sat down in the chair, grasping my hands and guided me onto his lap, straddling his hips. "You don't need to be scared or terrified, babe."

"I know it's irrational, but I can't help the way I feel." He placed his hands on my thighs and gently rubbed them.

"Start from the beginning, Sunshine. Start wherever it feels good to you."

I closed my eyes and tried to figure out where to start. I took a deep breath and let it out. "I emptied all my boxes today. Even the one I had in the den filled with all the crap I only use once a year. They needed to be empty because everywhere I've lived there's always been at least one box I don't unpack. I moved around so much with my mom that it only made sense to remove the things I needed and leave the rest in boxes."

"What about when you lived with Mark?"

I shook my head and laughed. "Nope. I had two boxes in the back of our closet that drove Mark crazy. He always nagged me to unpack them, but I never did. Unpacking meant I was there to stay and, even though I told him I would marry him, I always felt the rug could be ripped out from underneath me, taking everything away." I glanced away, the tears starting to fall. "And it did. Everything got taken away, and I had nowhere to run but here. To my dad. And then to you."

Troy wrapped his arms around my waist and turned my head to look at him. "So does you unpacking your boxes mean what I think it does?"

I reached up, feeling the days worth of stubble on his cheek and smiled. "My boxes unpacked mean that, even though I'm terrified out of my mind, I'm here to stay, and nothing is going to make me run."

"I don't think I've ever heard more beautiful words, baby girl." He tightened his arms around me and held me close.

"Do you hear that song?" I asked, ready for the next part of my plan.

Troy leaned his head back and listened. As Gwen and I were driving home, I had heard the perfect song on the radio. Lady Antebellum "I Run to You" was the song I was listening to on repeat for the last half an hour. Every word they sang rang true for what I felt for Troy.

"You running to me now, Sunshine?" Troy asked, a smile spreading on his lips.

"I've found there's no better place to run to." I climbed off Troy's lap and held my hand out to him. I pulled him off the couch, and he wrapped me up in his arms, swaying to the music.

I had never done something that felt so right before. Standing in my living room wrapped up in Troy was the greatest moment of my life. The only thing that made it better was when Troy quietly started humming, and his baritone voice singing the chorus to me.

I wrapped my arms tight around his neck and held on to the man who was going to forever be the one I ran to and never leave. We both raised the white flag, and there had never been a sweeter surrender.

--*-*-*-*-*-*-*

Chapter 31

TROY

"I love this song, baby girl, but how many times are we going to listen to it?" I laughed, tightening my hold on Marley.

Marley's body shook in my arms, and I leaned back to see if she was crying or laughing. "Thank God! I have had this song on repeat for the last forty-five minutes. I was ready to throw the stereo out the window before you got here," Marley laughed as she pulled out of my arms and turned the song off.

"Now, we need to talk about that dress, darlin'," I said, crooking my finger at her, beckoning her to me.

"Oh, you mean this old thing?" she laughed, twirling around, the dress floating around her.

"Here, now, Marley," I growled, needing her back in my arms.

She glided over to me, stopping a foot away from me. "Too far away," I whispered, grabbing her around her waist and pulling her to me. "I swore to myself the next time I saw you in this dress, I was never going to let you out of it."

"Oh, really?" she murmured, trailing a finger down my chest.

"Yeah, except now all I want to do is rip it off and devour you." My hand glided up her back, following the line of the zipper. My fingertips found the zipper pull and slowly unzipped it. With every inch of her back I exposed, the more she relaxed into my arms.

The only thing that was holding the dress up was her body pressed against mine. "I need to see you." She stepped back, her hand grasping the front of the dress. "Let it go, baby girl," I ordered.

Her eyes flared with lust, and she took another step back. "I think you need to work for it, Troy."

"I think we've both worked hard enough, don't you think so?"

She shook her head no and took another step back. "I've got a whole new outlook on life. I think the best things in life are worth fighting for. I did, after all, just win the Battle of Troy," she laughed.

"Oh yeah, the Battle of Troy, huh? So what exactly did you win?"

"You," she whispered. Her hand dropped, and the dress fell to her feet.

"Son of a bitch."

"Are you going to take your reward, Troy? I think we both won," she trailed her fingertips up her body and cupped her perfect breasts. "Except…" she trailed off, a playful smile on her lips.

"Except what?" I growled.

She giggled, the sound surrounding me, almost taunting me. "Except you have to catch me first." She winked at me and took off, running up the stairs, her laughter ringing out. I watched her perfect body running away from me, only a pair of panties and heels on and I couldn't move.

When she was half way up the stairs, she looked down at me and smiled. "You may have to chase me, Troy, but I can guarantee the prize is worth the chase." She winked at me again and finished running up the stairs.

I didn't need to be told more than twice. I toed my boots off, flipping them at the door and took off up the stairs, unbuttoning my jeans as I went. As I made it to the top of the stairs, I pulled my jeans off, tossing them behind me as I stumbled down the hall to her room. I pulled my shirt over my head and threw it on the floor. My socks came off last, balancing from one foot to the other. By the time, I made it to her bedroom all I had left on was my boxers.

I pushed open her door, and my breath whooshed out. She had the lights dimmed, candlelight the only thing illuminating the room. She was sitting on the edge of the bed, her legs crossed seductively, and waiting for me.

"Breath, Troy," she whispered.

I sucked air back into my lungs and knew right then and there that I was the luckiest man in the world. Never had I seen a woman more perfect. A woman who was going to be mine forever.

I walked into the room, not stopping until I had pushed Marley onto the bed and crawled up her body. My lips found hers, and I knew I was in heaven.

She sucked my bottom lip into her mouth, and I felt my dick turn into steel. Never had I had a kiss that could make me two seconds from cumming. "Slow down, baby girl," I murmured, pulling away.

"I don't want slow, Troy. I want you now, anyway I can have you," she whined, wrapping her arms around my neck and pulled me to her. Her lips devoured mine, taking everything I had. I grabbed her hands, clasping them above her head.

"Slow," I growled against her lips. She whimpered, wanting more.

My hand snaked down her body, cupping her sweet pussy. "This is mine." Her panties were wet with her need and my dick begged to feel her tight pussy. I grabbed both sides of her panties and tugged then down, tossing them on the floor.

"Troy," she moaned as I parted her pussy, seeing her clit begging for attention.

"Always ready for me, aren't you, baby girl?" I growled, leaning down, flicking her clit with my tongue. Her hips bucked, pressing her warm pussy into my mouth, begging for more. I grasped her hips, spreading her legs as far as they would go, giving me complete access to her sweet pussy. "I want you every way I can have you, Marley."

"Yes," she moaned as I flicked her clit.

"Flip over, baby girl. I don't think you know what I mean. I'm going to show you." I released her hips and leaned back, waiting.

"Hmm, no. Just keep doing what you were doing, please," she begged, her hands traveling over her stomach and spread the moist lips of her pussy open for me.

"Do what I say, baby girl, I promise it'll be good."

She stuck her bottom lip out, pouting, but did what I asked. "Get on your hands and knees," I ordered.

She slowly raised up, her ass wagging in my face. I ran my hand over the smooth globe of her ass and knew I was going to take her perfect ass. "You remember when I did you doggy style?" Marley nodded her head yes, tossing her head back, moaning at the memory. She kept her ass in the air, but dropped down on her forearms, knowing what I wanted her to do.

She spread her legs apart, revealing her wet pussy to me. I had access to her pussy just like before, but now I was going to take her to another level of ecstasy. "I'm not going to be able to do what I really want, baby because I don't have any lube, but it's still going to blow you away."

"Mmm, wait," Marley hummed, moving away from me and reached into the bedside table drawer. She tossed a bottle of lube at me and got back in the same position she was in before. She waved her ass at me, waiting. "Do it, Troy," she moaned.

I tossed the bottle of lube onto the bed, not ready for it yet. Who would have thought my sexy little Marley would have a bottle of lube next to her bed. My dick grew harder at the thought of spreading the cold lube over the tight hole of her ass, and I knew it was only a matter of time before every inch of Marley was mine.

Gently probing the tight rosebud of her ass, she pressed back into my finger. "You like that?" I growled. I reached down to her wet pussy, flicking her clit and I heard her groan, her head dropping to the bed.

I leaned down, opening the wet lips of her pussy and flicked her clit with the tip of my tongue. My finger probed the tight rosebud of her ass as I worked her clit with the tip of my tongue.

I grabbed the bottle of lube, leaning back and squirted a dollop onto her tight ass. "Troy," she moaned as I worked it into her. I squirted more and added another finger, stretching her sweet ass. She moaned low as I scissor my fingers inside her, my dick begging to feel her tight ass.

I leaned down, kissing the curve of her back, my fingers pumping in and out of her. I reached around with my other hand, flicking her clit. Her moans of pleasure surrounding me as I bring her to the brink. Just when she's about to explode, I edge off, wanting to save her ecstasy for when my dick is buried deep inside her.

"You think you're ready for me, baby girl?" I reached down, pulling my dick from my boxers and stroked my dick as my fingers plunged inside her.

Her head was buried in the pillow, her moans driving me closer to the edge. I pulled my fingers out, and she pushed back, trying to follow my retreating fingers.

"Just hold on." I grabbed the lube, coating my dick and squirting more onto her tight hole and tossed it on the floor. "You're mine, Marley," I vowed. I got up on my knees, positioning myself between her spread legs. She got up on her forearms and looked at me over her shoulder.

"I swear to god if you don't make me cum in the next five minutes I'm going to explode."

"Oh, baby," I growled, lining my dick up with her tight hole. "You're going to explode, just around my dick."

She pushed her ass into me, begging for more. I grasped her hip with one hand, holding her steady, controlling how fast this went. I slowly pushed into her, feeling the vise-like grip on my dick, each inch I sunk deeper.

Her breathing became short, shallow breaths and she buried her head in the pillow again. I stopped, halfway, giving her a moment to adjust. My dick begged for more, but I knew I needed to go slow.

I waited. Counting the seconds until she caught her breath.

--*-*-*-*-*-*-*

Marley

Troy was slowly killing me. I had never felt such pleasure with a bite of pain. It was intoxicating, and I wanted more. As he slowly pushed into me, I mentally chanted to myself to just relax. Halfway in he stopped, not moving. He was driving me crazy.

I caught my breath, knowing he was trying to take things slow, but my body screamed for more.

"You better not be done, cowboy."

"We're just getting started," he growled, leaning down, kissing me on my back.

"I need more," I pleaded, gripping the sheets.

He slowly pushed into me more. My body protested for a second and then relaxed, giving him access. He gripped my hips, his fingers digging in. He was on the brink of his control, and I was the one who was doing that to him.

He gave one last inch, and he was all the way in. "Son of a bitch," he bit off

I glanced over my shoulder, Troy's eyes clasped shut, "Give it to me," I moaned.

His eyes opened, connecting with mine. He growled low and deep and slowly pulled out. He pulled all the way out, leaving only the tip in and I felt empty. I pushed back, his dick sinking back in. "That's it, baby." He stayed still, letting me take control.

I slowly rocked back and forth, with every stroke the pain became less, and pleasure took over. He leaned forward, wrapping his arms around me, hands spanning my stomach. "You're fucking perfect," he growled, his lips inches from my ear. He trailed kisses down my spine as I kept rocking.

His hand snaked down my stomach, finding my clit. "Troy," I gasped, rearing back, taking him all the way.

"Faster, baby. Take it," he groaned, pinching my clit. I threw my head back, pulling out and slamming back into him.

My climax built, pleasure taking me over, only feeling. Our bodies became one, Troy pounding into me and my body milked him.

"So sweet, but so dirty," he growled when I reached down, pushing his hand out of the way, stroking my clit.

He gathered my hair, pulling it back with one hand, my head tilting back.

His hand grasping my hip while the other held my hair, giving me another bit of pain.

He slammed into me, and I pinched my clit, desperate for release. "Take it, baby, take it," he moaned.

My finger flicked my clit, pushing me over the edge as he slammed into me over and over. I pumped my finger into my pussy, feeling my tight hole pulse around my finger. Troy groaned above me, his fingers biting into me. He pumped his hot cum into me, filling me up.

"Fuck yeah," he groaned with one last thrust.

I collapsed onto the bed, completely exhausted but so good. Troy's still hard dick pulled out of me, and I gasped, feeling empty. We both panted, trying to catch our breath.

"Give me five minutes, maybe ten, and then your pussy is mine." He collapsed next to me, his arm thrown across me.

"I think I might need more than that. I don't even think I can roll over."

"I'll do all the work, baby girl." He brushed my hair out of my face and stroked my cheek.

"How the hell are you able to even talk right now? It's taking all my concentration to talk right now. I've never felt like that before."

"I don't think I'll ever get enough of you, baby."

"Hmm, well, when you put it that way I doubt I'll ever get enough of you," I scooted over, cuddling under his arm. "You're not going home tonight."

"I didn't plan on it." Troy turned on his side, pulling me fully into his arms. "I don't plan on leaving for at least a couple of weeks."

"What happens after a couple of weeks?" I asked, confused.

"King asked me to keep an eye on you."

"Why?" Mark's family was taken care of. What did Troy have to protect me from anymore?

"Leo Banachi is taking care of Kevin, Mark's dad, but King is still worried about the Assassins."

"But I have nothing to do with the Assassins."

"King just wants to be extra careful. He's struck a deal with the Banachi's to help take out the Assassins, and he is worried once the Assassins catch wind that the Banachi's are after them now, they might go after anyone connected to the Devil's Knights. You and I included."

"So you have no choice but to be with me again." Shit. Troy was obligated to be with me. He wasn't here by choice. I was a fucking idiot. I pushed away from him and jumped out of bed, grabbing the first shirt I could find.

I pulled it over my head, realizing it was Troy's. Shit, surrounding myself with Troy was probably not the best way to get away from him.

"What the hell are you doing?" Troy asked, looking at me like I was crazy.

"Why are you here?" I demanded.

"I thought we went over this. I'm here because I can't fucking be without you." Troy sat up and threw his legs over the side of the bed.

"No, you're here because you have to be. King asked you to look after me. That's the only reason." I couldn't believe what a fool I had been. I had poured my heart out to Troy, telling him my lame story of never unpacking all my boxes and now I found out the real reason he was here.

"What the hell? I planned on coming over here before King even asked me to keep an eye on you. I'm here for you, not for anyone else."

"How am I supposed to believe that!"

"Because I fucking told you, Marley! That should be enough." Troy stood up and pulled me into his arms.

"No, stop. I can't think when you touch me," I protested, pushing against his chest.

His arms tightened against me, and he wouldn't let me go. "Then I guess I'm going to have to keep my hands on you so you don't start thinking crazy shit, trying to run away from me."

"No! I can't believe I was such a fool." I closed my eyes, wishing I could take back the last two hours.

"Open your eyes, Marley." I turned my head away, just wanting to disappear. I shook my head no, and Troy grasped my chin, turning my face to his. "Open. Your. Eyes."

I had no choice. It was time to get the rejection over and move on. I opened my eyes and waited.

"I love you."

What? "You can't. You don't."

"I can, and I do."

"You clearly don't know me," I whispered.

"I've known you long enough to know I never want to go a day without seeing your beautiful face every morning I wake up. I refuse to let you run from me. I'll find you every time and bring you back to me and prove how much I love you."

I shook my head no, unable to talk. He couldn't love me. It was too soon. We shouldn't feel this way about each other. "I can't..." I whispered, the tears falling down my cheeks.

"It's ok if you don't love me, Sunshine. I just couldn't let you go on thinking that I was only here because you were some obligation to you. Hell, if Gravel threatened to kill me if I ever saw you again I would still be here. I want to be here, Marley." "

"I... I... I love you, too," I whispered.

"I don't want to live without you any more Marley. I can't do it."

"I love you," I mumbled. I wrapped my arms around Troy's neck, and he pulled me close.

"You really thought I was only here because I had to be?" he mumbled into my hair.

"Sorry."

"You are definitely going to keep me on my toes, Sunshine. I'm gonna have fun proving to you every day that I'm here to stay."

"You don't have to. I promise. I'll try to keep my craziness in check," I laughed.

Troy pulled back, holding me at arm's length. "I love your craziness, and I love you, Marley. Don't ever change anything."

"Nothing?"

Troy laughed, "OK, maybe knock off the whole doubting I love you thing but other than that, don't change anything."

"Not even my lack of cooking? I could have Ethel try to teach me."

"Nope. I cook, you can do the dishes."

I tilted my head to the side and wondered how I had managed to stumble into a more perfect man for me. He loved me, crappy cooking and all.

"Deal," I held my hand out, waiting for him to shake on it.

"Oh no, Sunshine. If we're gonna agree on something, it'll always be with a kiss." He knocked my hand out of the way and threaded his fingers through my hair, pulling me close.

"I love you, Troy. You made the battle worth the reward."

"As long as you're the reward, I'll fight every day for you, Marley. I love you." He kissed me. He kissed me with everything he had, and it couldn't have been more perfect.

--*-*-*-*-*-*-*-*

Chapter 32

TROY

"Ugh, Troy, wake up, you're phone keeps ringing," Marley moaned in her sleep, hitting me in the head.

"Easy, wildcat," I mumbled, rolling over. I grabbed my phone and saw King's number. "Shit."

"What's wrong?" Marley rasped out.

"I missed four calls from King."

"Well, freakin' answer it before it becomes five missed calls," she mumbled into her pillow.

I swiped right and put the phone to my ear. "Yo."

"Where are you right now?" King demanded.

"In bed. Sleeping. What the hell is wrong?" I glanced at the bedside clock and saw it was only two thirty. Any phone call in the middle of the night was never good.

"You need to get dressed and get your asses to the clubhouse now."

I instantly woke up. "What's going on?"

"Someone just tried to bomb Meg's house."

"Holy fuck! Is she alright? What about Remy?" I jumped out of bed and found my pants I had dropped at the top of the stairs.

"We're all fine. I want everyone at the clubhouse, though. You and Gambler were the only ones I couldn't get a hold of. Clubhouse, fifteen minutes."

King disconnected the call before I could say anything else. I pulled my pants on, walking back into the bedroom and saw Marley sitting up, the sheet pulled to her chest, a confused look on her face. "What's going on?"

"You need to get dressed and then try calling Gwen. We need to get to the clubhouse as soon as possible." I grabbed my tee I had pulled off Marley earlier and pulled it over my head. I spotted my socks at the door of the bedroom and grabbed them.

"Troy! Tell me what's going on!" Marley demanded, sliding out of bed.

"Someone tried to bomb Meg's house tonight. I have no idea how bad it is. All I know is everyone is OK. The only ones King can't get a hold of are Gambler and Gwen. Get dressed, now." I pulled my socks on and watched Marley frantically grab sweatpants and a sweatshirt and pulled them both on. She shoved her feet into a pair of shoes that looked like ballet flats and grabbed her phone.

"What if something happened to Gwen?"

"That's why you need to call her, Sunshine. No one has her number but you. I'm sure they are both just sleeping."

Marley fumbled with her phone, almost dropping it, and finally put it to her ear. "She's not answering."

"Keep calling her, baby. Let's go," I grabbed her hand and dragged her down the stairs with me. I grabbed my boots that were by the front door and pulled them on.

"She's still not answering, Troy. Oh my god. What if something happened to her?" Marley cried.

"Look at me, Marley." I grasped her chin and tilted her eyes up to me. "She is fine. There has to be an explanation. Gambler was watching her. He wouldn't let anything happen to her. Trust me."

Marley nodded her head, tears streaking down her face. "She's my friend, Troy."

"I know, baby, and everything is going to be fine. As long as you're with me, everything will be OK." I shouldn't have promised her that, but everything needed to be OK. I knew Gambler would never let anything happen to Gwen.

"I love you, Troy," she whispered.

"I love you, too, Sunshine." I placed a gentle kiss on her soft lips and grabbed my keys out of my pocket. "Come on, baby. We need to get to the clubhouse, and we'll find out more, OK?"

Marley nodded her head yes, and we ran out the door and climbed into my truck. I pulled her next to me, needing her close to me. She snuggled into my side, her head resting on my shoulder.

Her tears had stopped. "We've been through so much, Troy. We can make it through this, right?" she asked as I pulled out of her driveway.

"As long as you're next to me, Marley, we can make it through anything."

"Promise?" she whispered.

"I promise," I vowed. She clasped my hand, holding on tight.

"I believe you." She turned her head, looking at me. I glanced at her, seeing her trust and love shining up at me and knew that no matter what happened, everything would be all right. Even if it was the last thing I did. Seeing Marley happy was something I would fight for every day.

I had gone through the battle, and I'll be damned if my reward was going to be taken away from me.

Marley was mine.

--*-*-*-* -*-*-*

Chapter 33

Gambler

This woman was going to be the death of me.

The End

For now...

Coming Soon...

Gambler's Longshot

Devil's Knights Series

Book 5

Opposites attract, or so they say.
With Gwen constantly throwing sass and questioning every
word that comes out of Gambler's mouth, Gambler and
Gwen maybe the first couple to prove that saying wrong.
All Gambler wants to do is keep Gwen safe, and that's it.
He never expected the unwanted attraction and the need to
protect her no matter what.
Gambler's intentions may be true, but Gwen has learned
the hard way that things are not always what they seem.
Can Gambler persuade Gwen to take a chance on him, or
will all bets be off?

About the Author

Winter Travers is a devoted wife, mother, and aunt turned author. With stories constantly flowing around her, Loving Lo was the one story that had to get out (new ones are knocking on the door daily now).

Winter loves to bake and cook when she isn't at work, zipping around on her forklift. She also has an addiction to anything MC related, her dog Thunder, and Mexican food (Tamales!)

Winter has eight total books planned for The Devil's Knights series and the Skid Row Kings series coming summer 2016.

Made in the USA
Charleston, SC
12 December 2016